Lizzy was laughing,

her lips parted, her eyes alight with amusement.

Suddenly Brandon couldn't resist leaning toward her and touching his lips to hers, catching the sound of her laughter.

The kiss lasted no longer than the melting touch of a snowflake.

But it stirred the embers of a fire that had once burned more brightly than anything either of them had ever known.

Dear Reader,

Welcome to Silhouette **Special Edition** . . . welcome to romance. Each month Silhouette **Special Edition** publishes six novels with you in mind—stories of love and life, tales that you can identify with—as well as dream about.

And this December brings six wonderful tales of love! Sherryl Woods's warm, tender series, VOWS, concludes with Brandon Halloran's romance—*Cherish*. Brandon finally meets up again with his first love, beautiful Elizabeth Forsythe. Yes, Virginia, as long as there is life and love, dreams *do* come true!

Heralding in the Christmas spirit this month is *It Must Have Been the Mistletoe* by Nikki Benjamin. This winsome, poignant story will bring a tear to your eye and a smile to your lips!

Rounding out this month of holiday cheer are books from other favorite writers: Trisha Alexander, Ruth Wind, Patricia Coughlin and Mona van Wieren.

I hope that you enjoy this book and all the stories to come. Happy holidays from all of us at Silhouette Books!

Sincerely,

Tara Gavin
Senior Editor
Silhouette Books

P.S.—We've got an extra special surprise next month to start off the New Year right. I'll give you a hint—it begins with a wonderful book by Ginna Gray called *Building Dreams!*

SHERRYL
WOODS
CHERISH

Silhouette®

™

SPECIAL ▼ EDITION®

Published by Silhouette Books New York

America's Publisher of Contemporary Romance

SILHOUETTE BOOKS
300 East 42nd St., New York, N.Y. 10017

CHERISH

Copyright © 1992 by Sherryl Woods

ISBN: 0-373-09781-6

First Silhouette Books printing December 1992

All the characters in this book have no existence outside the
imagination of the author and have no relation whatsoever to
anyone bearing the same name or names. They are not even
distantly inspired by any individual known or unknown to the
author, and all incidents are pure invention.

®: Trademark used under license and registered in the United
States Patent and Trademark Office and in other countries.

Printed in the U.S.A.

Books by Sherryl Woods

Silhouette Special Edition

Safe Harbor #425
Never Let Go #446
Edge of Forever #484
In Too Deep #522
Miss Liz's Passion #573
Tea and Destiny #595
My Dearest Cal #669
Joshua and the Cowgirl #713
*Love #769
*Honor #775
*Cherish #781

*Vows

Silhouette Desire

Not at Eight, Darling #309
Yesterday's Love #329
Come Fly with Me #345
A Gift of Love #375
Can't Say No #431
Heartland #472
One Touch of Moondust #521
Next Time... Forever #601
Fever Pitch #620
Dream Mender #708

Silhouette Books

Silhouette Summer Sizzlers 1990
''A Bridge to Dreams''

SHERRYL WOODS

lives by the ocean, which, she says, provides daily inspiration for the romance in her soul. She further explains that her years as a television critic taught her about steamy plots and humor; her years as a travel editor took her to exotic locations; and her years as a crummy weekend tennis player taught her to stick with what she enjoyed most—writing. ''What better way is there,'' Sherryl asks, ''to combine all that experience than by creating romantic stories?''

The Halloran family requests
the honour of your presence
as Jason Halloran & Dana Roberts Halloran
and Kevin Halloran & Lacey Grainger Halloran
reaffirm their love
and renew their matrimonial vows
and
as Brandon Halloran & Elizabeth Forsythe Newton
enter a new life together.
Please share in their joy
at ten o'clock in the morning
on the twenty-first of June
at Whitehall Episcopal Church,
Boston, Massachusetts.

Prologue

Brandon Halloran had never felt so rich, and for once in his sixty-eight years it had nothing to do with the money or the possessions he'd amassed. Squaring his shoulders, his eyes misted over as he caught sight of his beloved Elizabeth at the back of the old Boston church he'd been attending for his entire lifetime. There was no denying the passage of time, but by God, she was a beauty still.

Petite, vivacious and with an undimmed sense of mischief in those twinkling blue eyes of hers, Elizabeth Forsythe Newton radiated joy as her gaze met his. Her pace picked up just a fraction—one beat ahead of the wedding march—as if she couldn't quite wait, after all this time, to be his.

Oh my, yes, Brandon thought, his own heart filling with anticipation. The wait had definitely been too long. Nearly fifty years had passed, during which he'd married another woman and raised a family. He'd seen his own grandson wed to a spunky girl who'd reminded him so much of his precious Elizabeth that his heart had ached.

Life had a way of making amends, though. Finding Lizzy again after all this time had made Brandon feel twice blessed. When he'd finally convinced her that they weren't a couple of old fools for wanting to get married at this stage of their lives, she'd tackled the plans with the enthusiasm of a young girl. She'd even drawn his beloved daughter-in-law and granddaughter-in-law into the celebration and convinced them to share the day by renewing their own vows.

His heart full, Brandon watched his son pledge to honor his wife. Kevin had almost lost that woman—twice, in fact. There'd been a time when Brandon himself had put obstacles in their path—one of his few regrets. He'd been convinced that Lacey Grainger wasn't the right woman for his son, that she'd been responsible for his rebellion against everything the Hallorans stood for. Only later had Brandon come to realize that Lacey was the mellowing influence, the gentle force that brought out Kevin's best instincts. To

Brandon's everlasting relief they had mended their marriage, and after today's ceremony of renewal, he expected it would be stronger than ever.

Now, impetuous, full-of-life Dana Roberts was another story. She'd led his grandson on a merry chase, starting things off by slugging Jason in a quiet, respectable tavern. Word of the ruckus had spread far and wide, to Jason's chagrin and Brandon's own delight. My, but Dana had been a breath of fresh air with her feistiness. She'd been a little rough around the edges, but Brandon had spotted the life in her right off, and he'd watched with glee as Jason struggled against the pull of her offbeat ways. Now they were expecting his first great-grandbaby—any minute by the looks of Dana.

Yes, indeed, he'd had a full and blessed life, Brandon thought. Maybe he'd been missing Elizabeth all this time, but the years hadn't been wasted if they'd all led up to this moment. Maybe Brandon and Elizabeth had come to appreciate what they had just a little bit more. Their path to the altar hadn't been easy. They'd had to learn all over again about trust and forgiveness, but he didn't have a doubt in his mind that it would be worth it.

When the minister turned to him, Brandon clasped Elizabeth's fragile hand and held on tight to quiet an unexpected attack of nerves.

"You are the light of my life," he told her. "We have missed so many years and yet it is as if they never were. What I feel for you today is as strong and as deep as it was on the day I first told you I loved you so long ago. Perhaps those words have even more meaning now that we have known the sorrows of loss, the strife of living, the meaning of forgiveness and the joy of rediscovery."

He raised her hand to his lips and kissed it. "I, Brandon, take thee, Elizabeth, a woman I loved and lost and have been blessed to find again to be my wedded wife. I promise to cherish thee all the rest of my days."

To his surprise there were tears in just about everyone's eyes when he'd finished. He wanted to whoop with joy himself, but knew he didn't dare. He'd caused the rest of them enough alarm over the past few months with his impetuous courtship of the woman who was now, at long last, his wife.

Brandon couldn't hold back a chuckle, though, as he thought of the way he and Elizabeth had shaken things up. By God, they had had a fine time. God willing, there was more to come—for all of them.

Chapter One

It had been an absolute bear of a day, with one last wintry rain to cast a pall over the promise of spring. Exhausted, Brandon Halloran poured himself a stiff drink and sank into his favorite leather easy chair in front of the library fireplace. As he stared into the dancing flames, he tried to empty his mind of all the problems that weren't up to him to solve. Unfortunately he didn't seem to be having any more luck with that now than he had over the past weeks.

He'd spent the whole day worrying anew about whether his son and daughter-in-law were going to patch up their marriage. A few weeks ago a divorce had seemed all but certain, but after Kevin's most recent heart attack, Brandon had seen for himself how much Lacey still loved his son. He couldn't imagine why the two of them were so darned blind to something that was clear as glass to him.

Brandon's hopes had risen when his son left the hospital. Kevin and Lacey had traipsed off to Cape Cod together. Brandon had been reassured that things were finally on the right track for the two of them. Then, just today, he'd found out that Lacey was back in Boston—alone.

He'd confronted her earlier tonight, only to have her remind him that he was butting in where he shouldn't. But if he didn't make them see sense, who would? He was family, dammit, to say nothing of being older and wiser.

It was nights like this that Brandon missed his wife the most. Grace had been good to him, loving and gentle. Given his mulishness, she'd also had the patience of a saint. And she'd known when to exert that iron will of hers to keep him from making mistakes he'd regret.

If he and Grace had lacked a certain passion, well, that wasn't the worst thing in the world. Before she'd died so suddenly two years ago, they'd raised a wonderful son and seen their grandson grow into a fine young man. Maybe it was good she hadn't seen Kevin's marriage hit this rough patch. Her heart would have ached just as badly as Brandon's did.

He and Grace had always been able to talk things through. That was the quality he missed the most. She would have understood this empty feeling in the pit of his stomach better than anyone. She'd always known what trouble he had letting go of anything, whether it was putting an end to the meddling in his son's life or walking away from the textile company he'd inherited from his father. How did these young people today say it? Get a life! That's what he needed to do, let go and get a life.

There was certainly no denying it was time to let go of the business he'd spent a lifetime building. He was sixty-eight years old. Thank goodness he still had his health. He could carry on at the helm of Halloran Industries another decade—at least that's the way he felt in the mornings with the whole day stretched out ahead of him.

The truth of the matter was, though, it was past time to give his son and grandson their chance. He'd first taught Kevin and then Jason the best he could, and now it was time to turn over the reins.

Maybe if he had a different personality, he could keep a hand in, stay in the background. He knew himself well enough, though, to realize that as long as he entered that building, he'd never be able to keep still about the decisions being made inside it. The only way for Kevin and Jason to put their own stamp on Halloran Industries would be for Brandon to walk away and not look back.

Damned if he knew how, though. What the devil would he do with all those long, lonely hours? Travel? What was the fun in seeing the world if there was no one to share the experiences with? He could read, play a little golf, but that would never fill up enough hours. His mind would atrophy in a month without the daily challenge of running his company, without the fun of finding some new fabric to design and work into Halloran Industries' line of quality textiles.

Brandon's "whims," Kevin and Jason called them. Yet those whims had kept their company thriving. They'd given him a reason to go on during the bleak days after Grace's death. He'd had some dandy adventures searching for ways to upgrade fabrics so that designers the world over would seek his company out for their richest, most sophisticated customers. The thought of giving all that up left Brandon feeling lost.

Well, he'd just have to make it work. It wasn't fair to hang on forever, not when his son and grandson had both long since proven their worth.

Brandon studied the scrap of paper he held in his hand and wondered if it had the answer.

Just before he'd left the office, he'd finally gotten a call from the detective he'd hired a few months back. Hiring the man had been an impulsive action, one of those spur-of-the-moment, middle-of-the-lonely-night decisions that didn't make a bit of sense in the cold light of day. Still, he'd gone ahead with it, caught up in a need to finally know, after all these years, what had happened to the one woman he'd never been able to forget. He was sure his beloved Grace would forgive him this bit of foolishness.

"Lizzy," he'd scrawled and then a phone number somewhere in Southern California. Elizabeth Forsythe Newton. It had been Elizabeth Forsythe when they'd met nearly a half century ago. Now, according to the detective, she'd been widowed five years, had two daughters and three grandchildren. She still taught school, substituting now, not full-time. She attended church on Sunday, went to an occasional movie. If there was a man in her life, the detective had made no mention of it. He'd promised to mail his complete report in the morning.

Brandon couldn't ask the detective the one question that was uppermost in his mind: did she remember those long-ago days they had shared, at all? Time blurred most things, but for him the memory of those days with Lizzy were every bit as vivid now as they had been hours or even weeks after they'd occurred. Not even a long and happy marriage had entirely erased thoughts of what might have been.

His housekeeper rapped on the door, then opened it. "Sir, your dinner is ready."

Another depressingly lonely meal, he thought and then made up his mind. "I know it's late, but can you hold it a bit, Mrs. Farnsworth? There's a phone call I need to make."

"Certainly, sir. A half hour?"

"That will be fine."

Even before she'd quietly closed the door, he reached for the phone and punched in the numbers before he could change his mind.

As the phone rang more than three thousand miles away, Brandon thought back to the summer day he'd first seen Lizzy, racing hell-bent for leather along a cliff overlooking the Atlantic. Her auburn hair caught the sun and gleamed like fire. Her white cotton dress had been hiked up daringly above her knees as she ran barefoot through the damp morning grass. He had been stunned by her beauty, but it had been the sheer joy in her expression that had captivated him.

The image lingered as the phone was picked up.

"Yes, hello?" a tentative female voice said.

Brandon's breath seemed to go still, as a powerful sense of déjà vu swept through him. The sweet, musical tone still held some little hint of bubbling laughter beneath the hesitancy. His heart, which had no business doing such things at his age, lurched and took up a quickened rhythm.

"Elizabeth Forsythe? Lizzy, is that you?"

He heard the faint gasp, then the whispered shock of recognition. "Brandon?"

"Yes, Lizzy, it's me. Brandon Halloran. Do you remember? It's been so long."

"I remember," she said, her voice sounding oddly choked. "You were the only one who ever called me that. Where on earth are you?"

"In Boston."

"How did you find me?"

He thought back to how hard he'd tried all those years ago, only to have her prove elusive. This time he'd taken no chances, spared no expense. "I hired a very smart detective."

"A detective? Oh, my. Why on earth would you do that after all this time?"

Elizabeth sounded nervous, maybe even troubled. It puzzled him, but he dismissed it as nothing more than the surprise of hearing from him out of the blue like this.

"Maybe I just wanted to hear the sound of your voice. You sound exactly the same, as if someone's just told you something that made you want to laugh. I've missed you, Lizzy. How are you? Are you well?"

He knew the answer to that much at least, but he was afraid it was far too soon to ask her the questions he really wanted to ask. Most important, he needed to know why she hadn't waited for him.

As they talked, hesitantly at first and then with their old enthusiasm, the years slid away. They were simply two old friends catching up. Haunting memories came back to Brandon as he listened, then were replaced by sorrow as she described so many experiences they hadn't shared.

"You've been out there how long now?" he asked.

"Since 1942."

"The year we met."

"Yes," she said softly. "The year we met."

Was there a note of wistfulness in her response? "Tell me about your life. You have children?" he asked, needing to hear her confirm every word in the detective's report.

"Yes, two daughters. They're grown now. The oldest, that's Ellen, is married and has three children herself. The youngest, that's Kate, has a real streak of independence. She claims no man will ever tie her down."

"Like her mother, if I recall correctly," he said, imagining another redhead with a fiery temper and the strength of her convictions. Brandon wondered if meeting Lizzy's daughters would be like traveling back in time.

Lizzy laughed. "She'd never believe you, if she heard you say that. She says she's not a bit like me, that I'm old-fashioned."

"That's certainly not the way I remember you."

He heard her quiet sigh and wondered at the faint hint of regret it held.

"Brandon, we knew each other for such a short time. I suspect neither of us remembers those days with much accuracy."

"But you have thought of them?" he prodded, waving off Mrs. Farnsworth's second attempt to call him to dinner.

"Some, yes," Lizzy admitted. "I can't deny that."

"What do you remember?"

"That we were very young and very foolish."

"That's not the way I remember it at all," he said. "I remember that we were very much in love, that from the first instant I saw you I was enchanted."

"I think it's best if we don't talk about those days, Brandon. A lifetime has passed since then." Her voice had cooled.

Brandon released a sigh. "So you do regret it. I'm sorry, Lizzy. I don't regret one minute of that time we spent together. I can't."

"Tell me about your family," she said in a sudden rush, as if she didn't dare allow his nostalgic note to linger. "You have children?"

He thought of refusing to be turned from the past to the present, then decided there was nothing to be gained from pressing her to look back. Not yet, anyway.

"I have a son, Kevin. He's taking over Halloran Industries soon."

"You're retiring?"

"I'm thinking of it."

"Somehow I thought you'd never walk away from that company. You always loved it so, almost as much as flying. Do you still collect fabric samples the way some kids back then collected stamps?"

"I not only collect them, I improve on them."

"Okay. Of course," she said, laughing. "I'd forgotten how self-confident you are."

"I suspect conceited is what you meant," he said, laughing with her. "Oh, Lizzy, how I've missed that sharp wit of yours. You never let me get away with a thing."

"It seems to me you got away with plenty," she said tartly.

The sly innuendo had Brandon chuckling again. That was the Lizzy of old, all right. She'd never been one to dance around the truth of things. He'd never known anyone else like her back then. Bold and sassy, she'd kept him constantly off balance, a rare occurrence for a man who even at eighteen had been pretty darned sure of himself.

"Lizzy, I want to see you again. I'll fly out tomorrow," he said, suddenly anxious to end a separation that never should have been. "We'll have ourselves a grand reunion. You can show me all the sights. Maybe we'll even go to Disneyland and pretend we're just a couple of kids again.''

Silence greeted the suggestion, then, "No. Absolutely not. I'm sorry, Brandon."

"But, Lizzy, we owe it to ourselves. For old times' sake," he coaxed. "What's the harm?"

"No, Brandon," she said, her tone suddenly cold and forbidding in a way it never had been before. "It's best to leave the past where it belongs, in the past."

The phone clicked quietly, cutting him off. He called back immediately, only to get a busy signal. He tried again and again throughout the evening, but by midnight he knew she wasn't going to take his call.

"Well, I'll be damned," he muttered, staring at the phone. No little slip of a woman was going to thwart his dreams. Not a second time. Surely if Lizzy remembered him at all, she remembered that he liked nothing better than the challenge of a chase.

For what seemed like hours, Elizabeth sat staring at the phone, the receiver defiantly left off the hook. No, she corrected. It wasn't defiance. It was sheer terror. Brandon Halloran made her feel things—crazy, impossible things—she hadn't felt in years.

A day ago Elizabeth would have sworn that her life was complete. She would have laughed at the thought that a sixty-seven-year-old woman's pulse could flutter at the mere sound of a man's voice. Gracious, the last time her heart had pumped this fast, she'd been on a dance floor doing a pretty spirited tango with a man wearing a polyester suit and too much shaving cologne.

She tried to imagine Brandon Halloran in polyester and couldn't. Cashmere or the finest linen would be more his style. She could recall, all too vividly it seemed, the way his skin had felt beneath her nervous touch. She absentmindedly picked up a magazine and fanned herself, then realized what she was doing.

"Elizabeth, you're an old fool," she lectured herself aloud. "What do you think you're doing dredging up thoughts like that? Your daughters would be shocked."

Of course, the subconscious wasn't nearly as easily controlled as she might have liked. She deliberately walked away from the off-the-hook phone, hoping she could forget all about the long-buried memories Brandon had just stirred to life, memories she had done her very best to forget.

Some, admittedly, were sweet and filled with a rare tenderness. Some were wildly wicked, which certainly explained the way her pulse was thundering. And others, the ones she needed most to remember, were filled with hurt and anger and a deep sense of betrayal.

Nearly fifty years ago Brandon Halloran had roared into her life, swept her off her feet and then vanished, leaving her to suffer the consequences of a broken heart. He had no right to think he could do the same thing again, not at this late date. Not even one word of apology had crossed his lips. Instead, the conversation had been laced with persuasive teasing, riddled with nostalgia. She was no longer a naive seventeen-year-old. She wouldn't give in to the smooth and easy charm a second time.

Elizabeth felt the anger mount and clung to it gratefully. As long as she felt like this, she would be able to remain strong. She would be able to deny whatever pleas Brandon made. She could ignore his coaxing, as she should have done so long ago.

Still and all, she wondered just a little about how he'd changed. Was he still as handsome and dashing? Back then he'd had a smile that could charm the birds out of the trees. It had certainly worked its magic on her. He'd walked and talked with an air of bold confidence. He'd had unruly blond hair that had felt like the silk that was spun in his factory. His piercing eyes had been the color of the ocean at its deepest—blue and mysterious. When his eyes lit with laughter—or desire—she'd been sure that what they shared was rare and certainly forever.

Believing all that, Elizabeth had been tumbled back to reality with an abruptness that had shattered her. Only by the grace of God and through the love of her parents had she been able to pick up the pieces of her life and move on. David Newton had played a huge role in that as well.

Her senior by ten years, David had been a fine man, tolerant and sensitive. And he had loved her unconditionally and without restraint. She owed him her thanks for seeing to it that she finished college, that she was able to enter a profession that had been more fulfilling each year. More than that, she owed him for giving her the very best years of her life, while asking so little for himself in return. She'd been content with their bargain, happy with the life they'd shared. Maybe there had been no glorious highs, but there had never been the devastating lows she'd known with Brandon.

Unlike David, Brandon Halloran had demanded everything and had very nearly cheated her of any future at all.

The ringing of the doorbell interrupted her thoughts. Suddenly realizing that she'd been sitting here in the dark for hours, she snapped on a light on her way to the door. When she opened it, she found Kate, flanked by Ellen and the youngest of Ellen's girls, fifteen-year-old Penny.

"Goodness, what a surprise!" she said, delighted by the distraction their arrival promised.

"Surprise?" Kate repeated, sounding miffed. "Mother, your phone has been off the hook for the past three hours." She marched into the living room and hung it up. "We've been worried sick about you."

"Kate's been worried," Ellen corrected. "We just came along as moral support. She said it was us or the police."

Elizabeth managed an astonishingly casual air, hoping to forestall too many questions. "Well, as you can see, I am perfectly fine. The cat must have knocked the receiver off when she jumped on the table. It's not the first time that's happened," she said, because she was not about to tell them about Brandon's call and the way it had shaken her.

Ellen regarded her speculatively, as if she could almost read her mother's thoughts.

"Mother, are you sure you're all right?" her oldest asked quietly.

"Certainly. Why wouldn't I be?"

"It's just that you look, I don't know, a little flustered. I've never seen you look quite that way before."

Her granddaughter peered at her closely. "Mom's right," Penny announced. "Are you sure you don't have some man stashed away upstairs?"

"Penny!" Ellen said sharply.

"Oh, Mom, don't act so shocked. Sex doesn't end just because you're over sixty."

"And just where did you hear that?" Elizabeth inquired, tucking an arm around her granddaughter's waist and steering her into the kitchen.

"It was in my health class. I could lend you the book, if you want."

"Penny!" Ellen exclaimed again with obvious dismay.

Elizabeth shot a grin at her daughter. "Chill out, Ellen." She turned to Penny. "That is the expression, isn't it?"

Ellen groaned. Kate looked from one to the other of them, her hands on her hips, her expression radiating indignation. "Well, I'm delighted you all find this so amusing."

Tension seemed to simmer in the air until Ellen gave her sister a hug. "Oh, come on, Katie dearest. Chill out. As you can perfectly well see, Mother's just fine. You were worried over nothing. You should be relieved."

"Why don't I fix us all some hot chocolate?" Elizabeth suggested. "The air's a bit damp tonight, don't you think?"

"Lace mine with brandy," Kate muttered, regarding the rest of them with a sour expression.

Elizabeth looked at her too-serious younger daughter and sighed. "I'm sorry you were worried, dear. I really am."

Some of the tension in Kate's shoulders eased. Finally she grinned. "Oh, what the hell. Let's go whole hog and order in a pizza, too. It's after nine and I just left the office. I missed dinner altogether."

"Now that's the spirit," Elizabeth said, noting that despite the long day Kate looked neat as a pin, every dark hair in place. What a contrast to Ellen's careless sandy hairstyle. "A large pizza with everything. I haven't eaten, either."

"Everything except anchovies," Penny countered.

"I happen to love anchovies, young lady. You can either learn to like them or pick them off."

Ellen and Kate shared an amused, conspiratorial glance at the familiar argument.

"You might as well give in kiddo," Ellen told her daughter. "Your grandmother will not budge on this."

By the time they'd finished the pizza, it was close to midnight. Elizabeth said good-night at the door and stood watching long after the taillights of their cars had disappeared.

She regretted worrying them earlier, but she was glad that it had brought them by, just when she needed a distraction the most. Now that they'd gone, the house felt empty and lifeless. It had never felt that way before. She'd never noticed the loneliness as she did tonight. Under the circumstances it was a dangerous state of mind.

For as long as Kate, Ellen and Penny were there, Elizabeth hadn't allowed a single thought of Brandon Halloran to creep in. Alone again, however, she knew that she had only delayed the inevitable. Brandon wasn't the type of man to be banished so easily from her thoughts.

To her dismay it seemed that that much at least hadn't changed over the past fifty years. He still had a way of capturing her attention and driving out all rational thought. She could only pray that some of that single-minded purpose with which he'd pursued her all those years ago had faded with age.

Chapter Two

Now that he'd found Lizzy, Brandon was not about to be thwarted in his campaign to arrange a reunion. What on earth could she find so threatening about a couple of old friends getting together to reminisce?

The next day he sent her two dozen pale pink roses, the day after that a huge basket of wildflowers. He followed up with rare orchids. The Beverly Hills florist was ecstatic over the lavish orders he phoned in daily. Brandon wasn't at all certain what Lizzy's reaction was likely to be. He figured it would be best not to call, to be patient and let her get used to the idea that he intended to become an important part of her life again.

It had been years since he'd courted a woman, but he knew the techniques couldn't have changed all that much. He would fill her whole damn house with flowers if he had to. Sooner or later she was bound to start chuckling at his extravagance. Then maybe she would experience a little twinge of purely feminine delight. By the time he exhausted the rare and exotic floral possibilities, he was hoping she'd cave in and track him down. Halloran Industries hadn't moved in nearly a century. She could find him anytime she wanted to.

Yet there were no calls, no letters as March gave way to April, so Brandon started sending extravagant boxes of candy. Lizzy had always had a sweet tooth. Half their dates had ended in a soda shop over hot-fudge sundaes. This time, though, a full week of chocolates produced no results. His patience started wearing thin.

Brandon was standing in front of a department store display of outrageously expensive French perfumes, totally at a loss, when Jason's wife sneaked up beside him.

"My, my, what are you up to?" Dana inquired, linking her arm through his.

He scowled at her. "How do you make heads or tails of all this?"

"Don't ask me. All those scents make me queasy."

He glanced at her swollen belly, which not even one of her boldly designed, loose-fitting sweaters could camouflage at this stage of her pregnancy. "Why aren't you and my great-grandbaby at home resting?"

"Because your great-grandbaby is coming in just a couple of months and I need to start buying things for the nursery."

"Nursery?" he said, readily dismissing the perfume as a purchase he could make later. "Let's go. I can help."

Dana stood stock-still. "Not until you tell me what you're doing surrounded by the most expensive perfumes in the store."

"Just looking."

His granddaughter-in-law rolled her eyes. "Come on, Brandon. You can't kid a kidder. Who's the woman?"

"Young lady, mind your own business," he said, trying to sound stern, rather than flustered. He'd hoped to keep all this to himself. He could swear Dana to secrecy, but that seemed slightly absurd given the lack of anything much to talk about in the first place.

She grinned at him. "Talk about the pot calling the kettle black. If you ask me in this instance, turnabout is definitely fair play. You started meddling in my life on the first day we met and you haven't stopped yet."

"I think it's time we had another one of those talks about respecting your elders. Even that rapscallion brother of yours shows me more respect."

Dana didn't look the least bit intimidated. "Save the lecture for the baby," she told him. "Maybe you'll be able to convince your new great-grandchild to worship the ground you walk on. I'm just plain nosy, especially when my single grandfather-in-law is showing all the signs of courting some mysterious woman."

"Looking at perfume does *not* constitute courting. I could be buying the perfume for my secretary."

"Oh? Is it Harriet's birthday? Is she the one you've been lavishing all those flowers on?"

Brandon glared at her. "What do you know about any flowers?"

"Just that last month's florist bill nearly put Kevin back in the hospital with another heart attack. You really should pay cash, if you intend to keep these things secret from your nearest and dearest. Kevin reads the fine print on every one of those invoices, remember?"

"I remember," he grumbled. Unfortunately he hadn't considered that when he'd placed the orders. "Are we going to look at baby things or not?"

"Sure," Dana said finally. "That'll give me that much longer to try to pry some real information out of you."

He waggled a finger under her nose. "If I weren't afraid you would go out and buy little pink sissy things for my great-grandson, I'd let you go alone."

"Your great-grand *daughter* may want little sissy things."

"There hasn't been a girl born into the Halloran family as far back as I can remember."

"Probably because nature knew what it would take to put up with the Halloran men. Now, come on. Let's look at wallpaper. I was thinking clowns. What do you think?"

"Clowns? Why not trains or boats?"

"How about little yellow ducks?"

"My great-grandson is not going to live with little yellow ducks," Brandon said indignantly. "He'll quack before he talks."

"Maybe we should look at cribs instead," Dana said. "Or diapers? Do you have firm convictions about diapers? I was thinking cloth because of the environment."

"Cloth is good," he conceded, then studied her worriedly. "Are you sure you should be doing all this running around? Maybe you should go back home and rest. Leave the shopping up to Jason and me."

"Not a chance. Now let's get moving. I have a list."

Dana dragged him through the department store at a pace only slightly slower than a marathon runner's. She found at least a half-dozen more opportunities to slip in questions about his social life. Brandon had to be quick on his feet to keep up with her and even quicker to avoid the verbal traps she so neatly set.

When they'd finally put the bundles into the trunk of Dana's car, he shot her a triumphant look.

"Thought you could wheedle it out of me, didn't you?"

She turned on her most innocent expression. "You mean the fact that this woman lives in California and her name is Elizabeth?" she asked as she slammed the car door.

Brandon stared at her in astonishment, then rapped on the window until she rolled it down. "How'd you know that?"

"Those invoices reveal a whole lot more than the cost of your flowers," she said smugly. "The word is out."

"If you knew all that, why'd you ask?"

"I wanted to watch you squirm," she admitted with a grin. "You've done it to us often enough."

Brandon couldn't stop the laugh that bubbled up despite his indignation at being caught. "I suppose you're feeling mighty proud of yourself?"

"As a matter of fact, yes."

"I wouldn't go getting too smug, young lady. There's still time for me to sneak my workmen into that nursery and paper the walls with itsy-bitsy footballs and baseballs."

"You do and your great-grandchild will be in college before you see her."

"You're mighty sassy," he observed with a chuckle. He leaned down and kissed her forehead. "Come over some night and dig around in the attic. There just might be an old cradle up there you could use.''

''Was it Jason's?'' she asked with an immediate spark of enthusiasm in her eyes.

''His and Kevin's before him. Might even have been mine.''

''Oh, I'd love to have that. I'll stop by.''

''Anytime you like. In the meantime, you take care of that baby.''

''Between you and Jason I don't have a choice.'' She backed the car out of the parking space, then called to him. ''Whatever's going on with you, I hope you're having fun.''

''Not yet,'' he admitted glumly, then brightened. ''But I expect to be.''

One week later Brandon packaged up a vintage recording of the song he and Lizzy had considered to be theirs—one of Glenn Miller's best to Brandon's way of thinking. He sent it overnight express. If that didn't get to her, he didn't know what would.

Sure enough, Elizabeth called that night just as he was getting ready to leave the office. ''Brandon, this has to stop.''

''Why?''

''I don't want all these gifts. Do you have any idea how overpowering all these flowers are in a five-room house? I feel like I'm sleeping in a garden.''

''Sounds romantic to me.''

"It might be, if I didn't have allergies," she grumbled, sneezing as if to prove the point.

Despite himself, Brandon chuckled. "Send the flowers to a hospital or a nursing home."

"Why are you doing this?"

"I told you. I want to see you. Why are you so reluctant?"

"I think it's wrong to try to go back."

It sounded to Brandon as if she'd wanted to say something else. The reluctance puzzled him. "We're talking dinner, maybe a little dancing. You always did like to dance, Lizzy. I remember the way you could waltz. I'll never forget the night we danced in that gazebo in the town square. I can still smell the honeysuckle. I loved holding you in my arms."

"No," she repeated, but there was less starch in her voice this time.

"You're weakening, aren't you? I'll be out tomorrow. Once I'm standing on your doorstep, you won't be able to resist."

"That's what I'm afraid of," she muttered.

Brandon waited as she drew in a deep breath. Finally, after yet another silence that seemed to last an eternity, she said, "I don't want you out here. I'll come there, Brandon. It's been a long time since I've been back to the East Coast."

"Tomorrow?" he said. "I'll call my travel agent and have her book you on the first available flight."

"You always were so impatient," she said on a breathless laugh. "Not tomorrow, but soon."

"Promise?"

"I promise. But I'll buy my own ticket, Brandon...when I'm ready."

He heard the determined note in her voice and knew she wouldn't budge. "I won't argue with you over the ticket," he said reluctantly. "But if you don't show up soon, I'll come after you, Lizzy. I swear I will."

That night, like so many others in recent months, Brandon Halloran lay awake staring into the darkness. Unlike those other nights, though, this time he was filled with excitement, rather than loneliness. He felt as if nearly fifty years of his life had vanished in the blink of an eye and he was an impetuous, daring young man again.

There was nothing that eighteen-year-old Brandon Halloran loved more than flying. From the day he'd graduated from high school he'd wanted nothing more than to join the Air Force and do his part in World War II. His parents had been appalled when he'd gone and enlisted rather than pack his bags for the Ivy League college that had accepted him. Now with his training complete and his orders for overseas in his pocket, he had ten days to say goodbye.

Unfortunately, every time he tried to say the words, his mother burst into tears and left the room. His father, who'd come to the United States as an immigrant from England, understood only that he was in some way responsible for Brandon's decision. He and his uncles had told Brandon stories about England from the day he was born. Because of those stories, Brandon felt this compelling need to fight in a war that was endangering their homeland.

Besides, he looked damned good in his uniform. Everyone knew that soldiers and fly-boys had their pick of women caught up in the drama of sending young men off to war. He didn't delude himself that what he was doing was part idealism and part ego. He liked the image of himself as a hero, liked even more the idea of flirting with danger.

"I'd rather have my son alive," his mother said when Brandon tried one last time to explain. She slammed a plate onto the kitchen counter with such force it shattered. Then came the tears and she hurried away, refusing to meet his distraught gaze.

His father came in just then. "You've upset your mother again, haven't you?"

"Dad, I don't know what else I can say to her."

"She's afraid for you."

"I'm good, Dad. I'll come out of this okay."

In a rare display of emotion, his father gripped his hand. "I hope so, boy. For all our sakes. She'll never forgive me if you don't."

"You do understand why I need to go, though, don't you?"

His father nodded. "If I were a younger man, I'd be going with you."

It had been more of a blessing than Brandon had expected. "I think I'll hitch a ride up the coast with a friend of mine for a couple of days. Maybe that'll give Mom some time to adjust."

"I think that would be best. Make the most of these days, son. Once you ship out, it's hard telling when you'll have another chance to relax."

Jack Brice picked him up a few hours later and they headed north. Jack's family had a place overlooking the ocean on the coast of Maine. Brandon had agreed to come along as much to cushion the blow when Jack told his family about his overseas orders as he had to relax.

When Jack broke the news the following day at lunch, his parents and sisters were every bit as stunned and dismayed as Brandon's family had been. After a while Brandon left them alone and went for a walk along the cliff overlooking the sea.

Even in summer there was always a stiff, chilly breeze blowing in hard from the north along there, but the sun beat down to counteract the cold. With his hands jammed in his pockets, he walked for the better part of an hour, thinking about the war taking place directly across the ocean that was splashing against the rocky coastline below.

He thought of the way the planes responded to his touch, the power he felt sitting at the controls defying gravity. And he thought of the reality of combat which up to now held no meaning for him. His mother, his father, the Brices, they were all right to be afraid. Hell, he'd be scared to death, too, if he allowed himself to ponder all the things that could go wrong on a mission. Fortunately he'd been blessed with an abundance of optimism. Hallorans made their own luck, and he intended to grab quite a handful.

Brandon was thinking about luck when he first saw the streak of white flashing past, a woman's bare feet kicking back, her hair streaming. The sunlight caught in the hair and turned it into fiery ribbons. He'd watched her run for no more than a heartbeat before the same compelling sense of fate that had drawn him to enlist sent him racing after her.

With his long, loping strides he could have caught up with her in no time, but he held back, enjoying the sight of her wide-flung arms, her bare legs, the way the white cotton dress clung to her curves.

He was so surprised when she suddenly whirled around and stopped stock-still that he almost ran into her. He drew up just in time to catch the bright spark of curiosity in her eyes, the faint sound of laughter on her lips. The run had pushed color into her cheeks and had her bosom rising and falling in a way that was all too provocative despite the demure style of the dress. Brandon felt his breath go still as awareness slammed through him.

Hands on hips, an arrogant tilt to her chin, she demanded, "Who are you?"

"Brandon Halloran."

"You don't live around here."

He grinned at her certainty. "I suppose you know everyone?"

"Every handsome man, at any rate," she said boldly.

Brandon had a hunch her daring tone was one she never would have used under ordinary circumstances. She looked as if she were trying it out for the first time, a little hesitant, a little defiant.

"Who are *you?*"

"Elizabeth Forsythe, which you would have known if you lived around here," she said smugly.

"I suspect you have a reputation with all the men for being outrageous."

She grinned in obvious delight at that. "Why, of course."

"How old are you, outrageous Lizzy?"

"No one calls me Lizzy."

"I do," he said matter-of-factly, enjoying the notion of standing out in her memory. "How old are you?"

"Seventeen," she said. "And a half."

"That half certainly is important," he said solemnly, all the while thanking all the gods in heaven for making her old enough for him to court.

She regarded him intently. "You're teasing me, aren't you?"

"No more than you're teasing me."

She turned away from him then and started walking. He fell into step beside her. "Tell me all about yourself, Lizzy Forsythe."

"Why?"

"Because I have a feeling we are going to be very important to each other and I want to know everything about you."

She glanced up at him with a look that was both shy and impish. "Now who's being outrageous?"

"We'll see about that," he said softly, wishing he dared to tangle his fingers in the silken threads of her hair, wishing he could see if her skin was nearly as soft as it looked.

"How long will you be here?"

"A week," he said. "Then I'm going to England."

"To fight?" she asked with a note of excitement threading unmistakably through her voice.

"Yes. Do you think a week is long enough for me to make you fall in love with me?"

She shook her head. "Not nearly long enough."

Brandon wondered how she could say that with such certainty, when he felt as if he'd been struck by lightning. There was no sense to the way he was feeling, no logic at all, just the gut-deep conviction that he'd finally met the woman with whom he would share the rest of his life.

He saw the strength in her and sensed that Elizabeth Forsythe could meet arrogance with confidence, passion with boldness. He knew intuitively that she was the sort of woman who could meet a man on his own terms. Making her fall in love with him might not be easy, but that would be more than half the fun of it.

Lying awake in the middle of the night nearly a half century later, Brandon sighed as he thought back to that time so long ago. How naive he'd been. And yet nothing that had happened in all the years since had changed the emotions that had filled his heart that day.

Brandon wondered if he would still feel that same sweet certainty when he saw Lizzy again. Maybe he was an old fool for wanting to tempt fate a second time, but he could hardly wait.

Chapter Three

Brandon waited impatiently for Lizzy to make good on her promise. There was a new spring in his step. He was actually humming an old tune—that Glenn Miller classic—in the office as he began planning in earnest for the retirement that had terrified him only a few weeks before. Kevin was back at work, his marriage on solid ground at last. Brandon finally felt he could leave Halloran Industries with his mind at ease. More importantly, he had something to look forward to.

Jason and Kevin clearly didn't know what to make of the change in Brandon's mood or the flurry of activity that accompanied putting his retirement plans into action. He caught their bemused expressions, the shake of their heads, more than once. It amused the hell out of him to keep them in the dark.

They probably thought he was getting senile—unless they'd added up the meaning of all those florist bills as cleverly as Dana had. Knowing Kevin, though, he'd probably only worried that there had been no line item in the corporate budget to justify the expense. Sooner or later he would grumble at his father for mixing his personal spending with the legitimate charges for Halloran Industries.

It was two long weeks before Lizzy's call finally came—enough time to plan, enough time to worry that she'd changed her mind, enough time to grow impatient.

When Brandon's housekeeper finally announced that a Mrs. Newton was on the phone, he was pacing the library like a caged lion, debating whether he ought to call her himself and put an end to this interminable waiting. Delighted he wouldn't have to make that decision, he grabbed the receiver before Mrs. Farnsworth had even left the room.

"Lizzy?"

"I'm here," she announced without preliminaries.

"Where?"

She named a hotel where they had once shared an intimate dinner. He wondered if she'd chosen it deliberately or merely because it was the only one she could recall when making her reservation. It pleased him to believe the former, rather than the latter, so he didn't ask.

"Alone?" he inquired with surprising hesitancy for a man who'd once been a daredevil fighter pilot and after that had commanded a large corporation and hundreds of employees for nearly fifty years.

Her sudden laughter seemed to float in the air between them. "You never did like to share, did you, Brandon?"

He knew she'd only meant to tease, but he answered the question seriously. "No, Lizzy, I never did. Not where you were concerned, anyway. You still haven't answered my question. Are you here alone?"

He feared more than he cared to admit that she would have packed up one of her daughters, maybe even the grandkids and brought them along as chaperons.

"Yes," she said, sounding satisfied that she'd taunted him into revealing a tiny hint of insecurity, "I'm alone."

"Then you'll come to the house for dinner," he said decisively. "I'll send a car at once. Can you be ready in ten minutes?"

Again she laughed, and he was transported back half a century to a time when life had been filled with possibilities and even minutes weren't to be squandered.

"Make it thirty minutes and I'll be waiting," she promised as she had then.

This time, Brandon thought, *nothing* was going to stand in their way.

Elizabeth stood in her hotel room for several minutes after hanging up the phone. It was just like Brandon to start making plans without giving her a second to think over her answer. Only just now had she realized how much she had missed that quick decisiveness, that rush of enthusiasm that spoke volumes about his feelings even when he couldn't say the words. A woman would always know where she stood with a man like Brandon.

If he'd had his way nearly fifty years ago, they'd have been married a week after they met. Truth be told, she'd wanted that as much as he had, but she'd been reared as a proper young lady and proper young ladies back then hadn't gone rushing off to get married on a whim, not when they'd barely turned seventeen and when the man was very nearly a stranger.

Brandon had coaxed. He'd wooed her with every bit of inventiveness at his command. He'd wanted to ask her father for her hand. She had believed in his love, but she was too cautious by far to give in, even to a handsome airman about to go off to war.

Even if she had been willing, her parents would have come between them. They had dreams for their only daughter and those dreams didn't include an impetuous marriage to a man heading straight into harm's way.

Nothing had stood in the way of her giving him her love, though. Right or wrong, Elizabeth had not wanted that regret weighing on her forever. There had been time enough later to consider that single, glorious night in his arms and all its implications in an era when nice girls definitely didn't go to bed with young men before marriage.

And she had paid for that night. Oh, how she had paid, but she hadn't been able to resent him for turning her into what her staid parents had called soiled goods. How quaint and unimportant that sounded in this day and age. At the time, though, it had seemed a calamity.

As she touched a bit of blusher to her cheeks and wondered what he would think when he saw her after all these years, she recalled the way he'd looked at her when she'd turned down his marriage proposal.

"You're saying no?" he'd said, his stunned expression reflecting the bemusement of a young man already used to getting his own way in everything that mattered. He'd counted on a splashy diamond ring to persuade her, but she'd refused to allow him to slip it on her finger. She was desperately afraid of being tempted to change her mind. It was difficult enough not to give in to the lure of an impulsive elopement.

"I'm saying no... for now," she'd told him gently, but firmly. "Our time will come when you're home again. I promise I'll wear the locket you gave me, every single day, and I'll be waiting."

She had meant it with all her heart.

But their time hadn't come. Brandon had gone off to England to fly daring missions that had terrified her more with each descriptive letter he sent. Those letters had reminded her how brave he was. Though he had thought her bold, she was weaker by far than he'd imagined. It would never have worked between them. Or so she tried to tell herself as the daily letters had slowly trickled down to one a week or less.

A few months later her family had left Maine and there had been no choice for Elizabeth but to go with them. They had made that clear, just as they had their feelings about Brandon. Brandon's letters had stopped altogether then. She'd been devastated, but not terribly surprised. Her parents told her over and over that he'd never loved her at all. She'd guessed he'd found someone else overseas, someone all too willing to make a commitment to a man with his money and charm and daring. Envisioning him with a war bride from England had hurt her more than she'd ever let on to anyone.

Resigned to never seeing him again, she had finally taken off the locket and relegated it to a box with other treasures. She made a safe, secure life for herself in

California. She'd married and taught school. Widowed now, she had two beautiful daughters and three energetic grandchildren, two of whom were already older than she had been when she and Brandon had met.

Just this week it had been Ellen, her oldest daughter, who'd found the gold locket with Brandon's picture in it sitting in a crystal bowl on the coffee table. Elizabeth had placed it there after looking at the picture inside time and again, trying to make up her mind about the folly of taking this trip.

"I've never seen this before," Ellen said as the fragile gold chain sifted through her fingers. The heart-shaped locket had rested in her palm.

Elizabeth reached for it, flustered and uncertain, but she hadn't been able to prevent Ellen from looking inside.

Her daughter had studied the tiny photograph for several minutes before looking up and saying quietly, "He's very handsome. Who is he? It's not Father."

"No," Elizabeth admitted. "It's someone I knew long ago, before I met your father."

Ellen studied her face for what seemed an eternity, then said with obvious amazement, "You loved him very much, didn't you?"

Elizabeth shrugged nonchalantly, but her pulse scrambled. "I thought I did, but I was very young."

"What happened?"

"I'm not really sure. He went off to war and we lost touch." It was the simplest explanation she could think of for something that had seemed so terribly complicated at the time. She managed to keep any hint of bitterness out of her voice.

"Were you engaged?"

"Not officially, though he wanted very much to marry me before he left. I turned him down."

"But why, if you loved him?"

Elizabeth sighed. "You can't imagine how many times I asked myself that same question. In the end, though, it seems I made the right decision."

"Why do you have this out now?"

"I heard from him a few weeks ago."

Ellen's eyes lit up at once, clearly fascinated. "Really? He found you after all this time?"

"Yes," she said. Then because she was still amazed by it, she added, "He hired a detective of all things."

"Oh, Mother, that's so romantic."

Romantic. Yes, that definitely summed up Brandon. Romantic and, as it had turned out, irresponsible. Elizabeth took the locket from her daughter's hand and ran her fingers over the simple design engraved on the face of the heart. It felt warm from Ellen's touch.

"I don't know what to do," Elizabeth admitted.

"He wants to see you. Is that it?"

She nodded. "And I promised I'd go to Boston, but now I'm not so sure."

"Mother, you have to go. You promised, didn't you? He doesn't sound like the kind of man who'd let you go back on your promise. Besides, what's the worst that could happen?" her dreamy, romantic Ellen said with stars in her eyes. "He's gotten fat and bald?"

Even now that she'd made it as far as Boston, Elizabeth could think of a dozen worse things than that, that could go wrong with such an impetuous trip. None of them had she dared to share with Ellen.

There was no denying, though, that she wanted to be here, wanted to see Brandon again, if only to resolve all the old hurts that she'd so carefully banked in order to get on with her life. Maybe now, at last, she could truly put the past behind her.

It had surprised Elizabeth that Brandon had sounded almost as nostalgic about their brief romance as she felt. If the memories hadn't faded for him after all this time, why had he let her go so easily? Why had he abandoned her?

Her heart still ached when she thought about the way she'd watched the mail day after day, only to be disappointed again and again, until finally it had become too painful to watch. Now she would ask him why. She would satisfy herself that she'd gilded the memory, that Brandon Halloran wasn't the romantic hero she remembered at all.

And then she would run back to her full, satisfying life in California and live out her days in peace. One last piece of unresolved business would be finally put to rest. Until he'd called, she'd had no idea that it still mattered so much to her to know what had happened.

So here she was, back in Boston for the first time in decades, her stomach tied in knots, her fingers trembling. Even at seventeen she was certain she'd never felt this giddy sense of anticipation.

Elizabeth ran a brush through the short hair that she'd finally allowed to turn gray. Oh, how she wished it were the same rich auburn it had been way back then. Brandon had loved her hair, long and touched with fire, he used to say.

When they'd made love on that one incredible moonlit night, he'd allowed the strands to flow through his fingers like silken threads, fascinated with it. What would he think of this short cap of waves that her daughters said took ten years off her age, despite the gray?

She smoothed her pale blue suit over hips that were still slender and adjusted the flowered silk scarf at her throat. Beneath the scarf she could feel the locket pressing against her skin, its once-familiar touch oddly reassuring.

Still, she was filled with trepidation as she went with the driver Brandon had sent. Were either of them prepared for the changes? Could they possibly avoid disappointment?

When the car drove up the winding driveway of the same impressive brick Colonial family home that she recalled from one brief visit years before, for one instant she wanted to turn back. She wanted to flee before illusions were shattered—or confirmed.

She wasn't sure which she feared more, the answers he would give or the disappointed realization that things between them could never be the same. Maybe it would have been wisest, after all, to keep the past in the past, where memories could live on untarnished.

Then the door opened as if Brandon had been watching impatiently for her arrival from just inside. He stepped outside into the glow of the brass lamps on either side of the door. Elizabeth's breath snagged in her throat as she allowed herself the freedom to study him unobserved through the limousine's tinted windows.

He was older to be sure, but he was just as tall and handsome as she remembered him. Like hers, his hair had gone silver, but it only made him look more distinguished in his dark suit. Any woman would be proud to appear on his arm. She had envisioned him once exactly like this—lean, sophisticated, impressive—back in the days when she spent too many hours imagining the two of them growing old side by side.

The quick, once-familiar flutter of her pulse took her back nearly fifty years and she knew that, in this way at least, time had stood still.

Chapter Four

At the first sign of headlights turning into the driveway, Brandon felt his pulse begin to race. He had the front door open, his heart thudding with anticipation, before the limousine could brake to a stop. It took every last bit of restraint he possessed to keep from sprinting down the steps. Instead he waited impatiently for his driver to open the door, more impatiently yet for Elizabeth to emerge.

For no more than the space of a heartbeat he was taken aback by the short hairstyle, the unapologetic gray that had replaced the stunning auburn he'd remembered. Then he looked at her tanned face, the way the sassy style emphasized her unchanged, twinkling eyes and admitted that the short cut, even the gray, suited her.

He noted that her legs, as she swung them out of the car, were still slender, her figure still girlish in a sedate blue suit with a twist of something silky at her throat. By golly, she was still a looker all right.

Brandon thought back to the snapshot he'd carried off to war. It had shown off that figure. She'd worn white shorts and a skimpy top that tied behind her neck and at her waist. The provocative outfit had left her legs and back bare and gave the impression of height far taller than her actual five foot-two. She'd been glancing over her shoulder at the camera, Betty Grable pinup style.

He had pulled that picture out a dozen times a day, considering it his good luck talisman. Only after she'd stopped writing and vanished had he angrily torn it into shreds and thrown it away. The memory had lingered for far longer, along with regrets for his brash, ill-considered act.

He pushed the memories aside and went to meet her, holding out his hands. "Lizzy," he said, his gaze meeting hers, detecting the nervousness behind the brave smile. "It's wonderful to see you."

Her hands were like ice in his. She glanced at him far more shyly now than she had on the day they'd met, though her words were calmly gracious.

"Brandon. It's good to see you, too. You look well," she said.

"I'm better, now that you're here." He tucked her hand through his arm and led her inside. "I'm afraid I've rushed the housekeeper. She already has dinner on the table. Do you mind if we go straight in?"

"Of course not," she said, sounding surprisingly relieved.

He wondered if she'd feared the idle moments before the meal as he had, if she'd worried that conversation would lag, if she'd dreaded an endless evening begun in hope and ending in disappointment? How could a man who'd entertained politicians and celebrities in his time be so nervous about an evening with someone he'd once thought he knew even better than himself?

The elegant Queen Anne table in the formal dining room had been set for two with the finest Halloran china and crystal, brought over by his father from England at the beginning of the century. Candles glowed. A bottle of Brandon's best vintage wine was ready to be poured. White roses, opened just enough to scent the air, had been arranged dramatically in a crystal bowl in the center of the table. Even with such short notice, Mrs. Farnsworth had outdone herself. Although, she had told him with an indignant huff, no thanks to his agitated hovering.

Even with those exquisite touches, all Brandon noticed was the shine in Lizzy's eyes. She'd always had a twinkle in those eyes, a daring glimmer that belied her cautious nature.

Obviously, daring had overcome caution to bring her back to Boston, to bring her here tonight. He wondered why she'd been so reluctant in the first place. This wasn't some silly blind date she'd had cause to fear. But there'd been no mistaking the earlier reluctance, no ignoring the hesitation even now, a hesitation that he was certain went beyond simple nervousness.

Still he pushed curiosity aside and went through the motions of settling her in the chair next to his. He wasn't about to relegate her to the far end of a table big enough for Halloran family reunions.

Brandon's own meal cooled, untouched, while he listened to Elizabeth fill in the gaps they hadn't covered on the phone. More than the details, he heard the humor, the love, the fulfillment, and regretted more than he could say that he hadn't been the one to share them. How he wished that he'd been there to witness the shift from youthful impetuosity to mature strength, that he'd been the one to bring her laughter and contentment.

"Tell me about your husband," he said.

"He was a wonderful man, kind, thoughtful, generous. The girls adored him, especially Kate. She came along late, when we weren't sure we'd have another child. He doted on her. I wasn't sure what would happen to her when he died. For a long time she seemed almost lost without him."

"He made you happy, then?" Brandon asked, hiding the resentment that crept over him. It was foolish to be jealous of a man he'd never met, a man who'd been dead for five years. Yet knowing that didn't stop the pangs of regret.

"Very," she said.

Brandon regarded her speculatively, trying to interpret the note of determination in her voice, the defiant gleam in her eyes. "And love, Lizzy? Did he love you?"

"Perhaps more than I deserved," she said.

"What an odd way to put it."

"Don't you find that in relationships more often than not one partner cares more than the other, that one gives and the other takes? What about in your own marriage?"

Pained that she had hit upon something he had thought more than once about his relationship with Grace, he nodded. "I suppose that's so, about relationships, I mean."

"And your own?" she prodded, her gaze relentlessly searching his.

He felt it would be a betrayal of Grace to admit that she had loved more than he, yet he couldn't bring himself to lie. "I suppose we found a balance," he said finally, skirting the truth of it. There had been a balance of sorts. He didn't think his wife had ever felt cheated. He had cared deeply for her, honored their vows, and to his dying day he would be grateful for the life they had shared, the son she had borne him.

"Tell me more about your life in California," he said at last.

He sat back, then, and listened, watching the way laughter put such sparks in her eyes, the way her face became animated when she talked about her daughters and grandchildren. Then there was no mistaking the radiance of love, which proved he'd been right when he'd guessed she hadn't felt it nearly so deeply for her husband.

Finally, when she'd been talking nonstop for some time, Elizabeth lifted troubled eyes to his. "You've been awfully quiet, Brandon. It's not like you."

"I like listening to you. I've had too many quiet meals in this room over the past couple of years. It's wonderful to have some laughter in here again."

"Then why do you look so sad?"

"I suppose I was thinking about how much I missed."

She looked startled by the candid answer. "Don't try to make me believe you haven't had a good life," she chided. "You're not the sort of man to let life pass you by."

"No, I've had a wonderful life," he admitted. He told her about his business triumphs and his family, omitting the inexplicable emptiness that had nagged despite everything. He wouldn't have her thinking him ungrateful for all the genuine blessings in his life.

"The years since Grace died have been lonely, though. These past weeks I've been thinking how much I wished I had someone to share things with again."

"You're a handsome, successful man, Brandon. I'm sure there are dozens of women who'd be pleased by your attention."

It was odd, but he'd never really thought of that before. He supposed it was true enough. There had been invitations to dinners, the symphony, the ballet, charity affairs. He'd even accepted a few, but always in the back of his mind he must have been waiting for his search for Lizzy to be successful. He hadn't seriously considered any of those other women as candidates for his affection.

Brandon gazed solemnly into Elizabeth's eyes and took her hand. "I think fate has done it again, Lizzy. I think there was a reason for my finding you after all this time. Not a woman I know could hold a candle to you."

"And I think you've had too much wine to drink," she retorted, but there was a becoming blush of pink in her cheeks and she didn't withdraw her hand.

"Don't pretend you don't know exactly what I mean. You didn't come all this way just to say hello, did you?" he countered, watching the blush deepen.

"Of course not," she said hurriedly. "It's been years since I've seen Boston."

"Are you trying to say that I'm just one of the sights on your schedule?" he teased. "I'm old, Lizzy, but I'm not a monument."

"You still have a sizable ego, I see."

"You'd never want a man who wasn't sure of himself."

"And how would you know that?"

"No one changes that much, not even in a lifetime."

"Perhaps at my age I'm not even looking for a man," she said. "Did you consider that?"

"Then you're here for nothing more than a little talk about old times?"

"Yes," she said, but there was something wistful in her voice that touched his heart and told him the quick response wasn't quite the truth. She needed more than memories, the same way he did. Just thinking about proving that to her made his tired old blood pump a little faster.

"And maybe some answers," she added determinedly then, not quite meeting his gaze as she withdrew her hand from his. She folded her hands together as if to keep them from trembling. Her knuckles turned white and there was a sudden frost in her voice.

"Answers?" he asked warily, startled by the shift in her mood.

She looked up then, her gaze colliding with his. "What happened back then, Brandon?" she asked indignantly. "Did you meet someone else? Did you forget I was waiting? Explain it to me. I think you owe me that much."

Stunned by the sudden burst of anger over hurts a half century old, he simply stared at her. "Forget you? Never, Lizzy. Never!"

He hit the table with his fist and suddenly he was every bit as angry as she, drawing on emotions he'd thought dead and buried long ago. He shoved his chair back and stood, towering over her. She never even flinched, though her hands clenched even more tightly.

"How could you even ask something like that?" he demanded.

"Then why did the letters stop?"

"I could ask you the same thing," he shot back. "For weeks after I got your last letter, I kept on writing. Not a day passed that I didn't write some little note at least. Do you know what it's like being away from home, alone?" He held his fingers a scant inch apart. "This close to dying every single day, only to think that the woman you love more than life itself has forgotten all about you so quickly?"

"But *I* wrote," she swore just as vehemently. "It was *you*. I never got any letters, not after we moved."

Suddenly they stopped and stared at each other as the meaning of the furious words sank in. Brandon sank back into his chair as he realized that trust, as much as anything, was at stake. Either or both could have been lying.

To his regret, he saw that there was no way of proving what they said, not after all this time. There was no way of knowing for certain if the letters had simply been misdirected, lost in the chaos of war, destroyed by her parents—or never sent in the first place.

"We'll never know," she said finally, her voice filled with a sadness as deep as his own as she came to the same realization. "Will we?"

Brandon couldn't bear the uncertainty he saw in her eyes, heard in her voice. "You must believe me," he insisted. "I sent those letters. I swear I did. When I was injured and sent home, I moved heaven and earth to try to find you, but it was as if you'd vanished without a trace."

"You were injured?" she said, her eyes wide. "How seriously? What happened?"

"I'd only been there a few months when my plane went down. I got out with no more than some broken bones, but it was enough to get me sent home."

"So my letters could have gone astray?" she said slowly.

"Yes, as could mine."

He hoped she could see the truth in his eyes, could read the bitter agony of loss on his face. If only he'd hired a qualified detective back then, rather than counting on unreliable acquaintances in Maine and eventually in California. Leads had dwindled, then turned cold. By the time Grace had been introduced and encouraged as a suitable match, he had only discouraging answers. Grace had been there during the recuperation, not Lizzy. They had been, at the least, compatible. With no word on Lizzy, the choice had seemed clear.

"Only then did I give up," he swore. "That's the truth, Lizzy. You must believe me."

But rather than unqualified trust, all she said was, "I want to, Brandon. I want to believe you."

"We have another chance. Let's not let it go so easily this time," he urged. "Please, Lizzy. We're too old for more regrets. Say you'll stay and give me a chance to make it all up to you. We'll do all the things we never got to do back then."

For the longest time she looked indecisive, avoiding his eyes. Finally she said simply, "A few days, Brandon. I'll stay on for a few days."

There was an implied finality to the limit she set that nagged at him, but for the moment at least he would take what she was willing to give. He trusted in his own persuasiveness to see that a few days turned into weeks,

then months and eventually a lifetime. He could explain his determination no more clearly now, than he
could have decades ago. He only knew what he felt in
his heart. It was there again, beating with the same
strong certainty that had guided everything he did.

The phone in her hotel room was ringing when Elizabeth walked in, still shaken by the powerful emotions
that had gripped her from the first instant she had seen
Brandon again. It was after midnight, three hours earlier in California. She had no doubts at all that it was
Ellen calling to see how this first meeting had gone.

Desperately needing the sense of grounding that a
talk with her daughter would provide, Elizabeth kicked
off her shoes as she reached for the phone.

"Hey, Grandma, how was the hot date?" Penny
asked. Obviously she'd pried the information about
Brandon out of her mother and wanted details.

"We had a lovely dinner," she said primly.

"Boring," Penny pronounced. "Where'd you go?
Some real fancy restaurant?"

"His house."

"Better," the teen decreed. "Did he ask you to stay
over?"

"I'm here, aren't I?"

"That doesn't mean he didn't ask."

Elizabeth held back a chuckle as she heard a muf-
fled discussion on the other end, then Penny's dis-

gusted, "Hold on, here's Mom. Don't tell her any of the juicy details. Save 'em for me."

"There are no juicy details," Elizabeth said, wondering precisely when Penny had become so precocious. Maybe it was the result of being the youngest by nearly ten years, a delightful, much-loved surprise who, because she'd always had the company of those older than she, had grown up too fast by far.

"Okay, Mom," Ellen was saying, "let's cut to the chase. Is he bald?"

As Elizabeth settled herself on the bed, propped up by pillows, she thought of Brandon's thick silver hair. "Hardly."

"Fat?"

She recalled his trim body, which still did astonishing things for a custom-tailored suit. "Nope."

"Was that old zing still there?"

"For him or for me?"

"You're being evasive," Ellen accused. "That must mean it was there in spades."

"He is a very attractive man," Elizabeth conceded, regretting that she still felt that way about him despite everything. "Quite dashing, actually."

"And you're a gorgeous woman."

"A gorgeous *old* woman," Elizabeth corrected. "Stop talking foolishness. How's everything out there?"

"About the same as it was when you left here this morning," Ellen said dryly. "Don't try to change the subject. When are you seeing him again?"

"Tomorrow. We're going sight-seeing."

"And then?"

"And then I'm coming back to the hotel and going to bed."

"Oh, really?"

"Alone, Ellen. Alone," she said emphatically, but she couldn't help the feeling of anticipation that rushed through her as she considered the possibilities. She really was an old fool, she thought as the heat of embarrassment climbed in her cheeks.

"Sweetie, I'm awfully tired. I'll call you in a few days."

"Mom, you sound funny," Ellen said, her tone suddenly serious. "Are you sure you're okay?"

"Just tired."

"And a little nostalgic?"

"A lot nostalgic," she admitted with a rueful chuckle. "I think I'd better sleep it off."

"Mom, if there's still something special with this man after all this time, go for it. Okay? Promise?"

"Good night, Ellen," she said deliberately and slid the phone back into the cradle. She wasn't ready yet to dissect all the feelings that had crowded in after seeing Brandon for the first time.

There was no denying that the thought of him moving heaven and earth to find her at this late date appealed to her sense of romance, just as it did to Ellen's and Penny's.

Kate—practical, down-to-earth Kate—would be appalled that Elizabeth had even spoken to a man who'd betrayed her, much less flown clear across the country to see him. Kate held on to hurt, too long by Elizabeth's standards. She'd never gotten over the awful man who'd thrown her over. Ellen was more like Elizabeth herself had been five decades ago, willing to throw caution to the wind, especially when it came to her heart.

What Elizabeth needed now was a good strong dose of Kate's tougher nature. Something told her if she didn't cling for dear life to rational thought, Brandon Halloran was going to sweep her off her feet all over again and that was the very last thing she could allow to happen. She'd meant to put the past to rest. Instead it seemed she'd merely stirred cold ashes back to flame.

Just a few days, she promised. She would indulge herself in some old dreams, allow herself the rare thrill of feeling desirable again. She deserved one last rollicking fling. Then she would don a shroud of common sense and go back to California with enough memories to carry her through the rest of her days.

Chapter Five

Brandon knew he should have expected the commotion that followed his call to the office in the morning, but he hadn't. Within minutes of telling his secretary that he wouldn't be in, first Kevin and then Jason called.

"Are you okay, Dad?" Kevin asked. "Harriet told me you called and said you weren't coming in today."

"Maybe I just thought you ought to get used to running things without me. I am retiring, remember?"

The comment was greeted with a heavy silence. Finally Kevin said carefully, "We haven't even talked about that. Are you sure you've given the idea enough thought? It seems to me you decided that all of a sudden.''

''It was hardly sudden. You and Jason have been chomping at the bit to do things your own way for the past couple of years. I'd say it's past time for me to let you.''

''We're not trying to shove you out, Dad.''

''Hell, you think I don't know that? I just decided it was time to develop some new interests while I have time.''

''While you have time,'' Kevin repeated slowly. ''What's that supposed to mean? Dad, are you okay?''

''I think that's how this conversation started. I'm fine. I'm taking the day off because I have things to do. I can't recall the last time I took a long weekend.''

''Neither can I. That's why I'm worried.''

''Well, stop making such a fuss about it. I may even take the whole danged week off next week,'' he said irritably.

''Dad!''

Brandon ignored the note of alarm in Kevin's voice and hung up. Five minutes later he went through essentially the same conversation with Jason. At this rate he'd never finish his first cup of coffee, much less the once-fluffy scrambled eggs that had turned cold and hard while Kevin and Jason carried on about nothing. When a man got eggs only once a week, it was infuriating to see them ruined. He would never convince

Mrs. Farnsworth he ought to have them again another morning. She was as rigid with his diet as any chef at some fancy health spa.

He regarded the eggs ruefully, muttered a curse and poured himself another cup of coffee. Decaf, but at least it was still hot.

He figured Kevin and Jason weren't done with their questions yet, but he rushed through the paper in an attempt to evade whatever meddling they were likely to do.

Unfortunately he wasn't fast enough. He was on his way out the front door when Dana's sporty little car screeched to a halt in front of him, kicking up gravel. She hauled her bulky form out. It was evident from the haphazardly chosen clothes, the lack of makeup and the mussed hair that she'd been roused from sleep and sent over here on the double to check up on him.

Hands on hips, Jason's wife looked him over from head to toe. "You don't look sick," she pronounced.

"Never said I was."

"But Jason—"

"Is an astonishing worrywart for someone his age. Maybe if he had a couple of babies to keep his mind occupied, he wouldn't carry on so about me."

Dana grinned at him and patted her belly. "I can't make this baby come a minute sooner just to keep my husband off your back," she said. "Where are you off to?"

"I'm going sight-seeing, not that it's any of your business."

"Sight-seeing? Is there any part of Boston you haven't seen a hundred times?"

"I'm taking an old friend on a trip down memory lane."

Clearly fascinated, Dana said, "I don't suppose you'd want company."

"You suppose right. Now get on about your business and tell that husband of yours next time he wants to check up on me, he should do it himself."

"And have you pitch a fit because he's away from his desk? Besides, I worry about you, too, you know."

Brandon squeezed her hand. "There's no need, girl. I'm better than I've been in a very long time."

She nodded. "I can see that. In fact, you look downright spiffy. I can't recall ever seeing you in anything but a suit on a weekday." She smoothed his blue cashmere pullover across his shoulders. "Must be a woman involved. I don't suppose that mysterious Elizabeth from California has anything to do with your dapper attire?"

"Have I mentioned that you're a nosy little thing?"

"More than once," she said. "Just giving you a taste of your own medicine."

"I'll reform," he vowed.

"And pigs will fly," she retorted as she gave him a kiss on the cheek. "Wherever you're off to, have fun."

"I intend to." He waggled a finger under her nose. "And don't you go sneaking around trying to see what I'm up to."

"I wouldn't dream of it."

Brandon eyed the sporty little convertible Jason had given her on their wedding day. Dana had adamantly refused a new car, so his grandson had given her his, then bought himself a new one. It was an interesting compromise. Brandon made note of the technique. It might come in handy with Lizzy.

"I don't suppose you'd like to trade cars for the day?" he asked.

Dana's mouth dropped open. "You're kidding?"

"Nope. I think a ride in a convertible on a beautiful spring day is just what I need to impress..." He hesitated.

"Impress who?" she taunted.

"Someone."

"If you want my car, you're going to have to do better than that."

"No wonder Jason thought you were one tough cookie," he grumbled. "Okay. You've got the name right. It's Elizabeth."

"I already knew that much."

"Take it or leave it."

"I get the Mercedes for the day?"

"Yes."

"I'll take it. It's getting harder and harder to squeeze myself behind the wheel of my car." She exchanged her keys for his and sauntered over to the luxury car his driver had brought around earlier. She ran her hand lovingly over the metallic gray finish, then shot him a look that had him thinking maybe the exchange had been made too hastily.

"Drive carefully," he said, suddenly recalling the way she tended to take curves as if she were on the Indy 500 course.

"I should be saying that to you. If you put even a tiny little scratch on that car Jason gave me, you'd better trade it in on a new model on the way home. He might have put the title in my name, but he still considers that car his baby."

"As long as I don't catch sight of you in the rear-view mirror, I'll be just fine," he warned.

"No problem," she promised.

"Let me see those fingers," he ordered. "You got any of them crossed?"

"Nope," she said, laughing as she held out her hands for his inspection. "I'm as good as my word."

Brandon wasn't so sure her promise was worth spit, but she did take off and he didn't see any sign of his Mercedes as he drove into town to pick up Lizzy.

Lizzy was waiting for him in front of the hotel. She took one look at the flashy little car and a smile spread across her face. "Don't tell me this is yours?"

"I borrowed it from Jason's wife. Do you mind the top down?"

"On a day like today? Absolutely not. One of the advantages to short hair is that I don't need to worry about a little wind. Where are we going?"

"I thought a leisurely drive so you could get your bearings, then maybe lunch at Faneuil Hall Market-place. If you haven't been back to Boston in years, you probably haven't seen what they've done to it."

Lizzy sat up just a little straighter, her eyes alight with curiosity. With the trees budding new green leaves, the sky a soft shade of clear blue and just a handful of clouds scudding overhead, it was the perfect spring morning, one of Boston's finest.

Brandon felt rejuvenated at Elizabeth's exclamations of delight over everything she saw. It was as if he were seeing his beloved city through new eyes. Because she'd taught American history, Lizzy knew as much if not more than he did about the significance of many of the sights. She imbued the telling with a richness of detail and a liveliness that suggested what a magnificent teacher she must be.

"You've got to meet Jason's young brother-in-law while you're here," he told her. "He'd be fascinated by your stories. Sammy's not much for learning from books, but the boy has a lively mind. It came tragically close to being wasted."

"So many of them do," she said sadly. "It breaks my heart to see youngsters today graduating without the skills they need to make a go of it in today's world. There's no combatting crowded classrooms, the gangs and violence in so many cities. It's a wonder some of them get out alive, much less with any education."

"You're still teaching?"

"Substituting. In many ways that's the most frustrating of all. I go into a classroom not knowing the children. I see how they struggle. Maybe, if the teacher's out a week or more, I can see some tiny sign of progress and then it's over. I never know if they build on what I've been able to teach them, or if they simply go on muddling through."

"It sounds frustrating."

"It is. But I love being in the classroom so much that I wasn't prepared to give it up entirely."

A sudden thought struck him. "Why don't you found a school, Lizzy? A special one for the youngsters with disadvantages who could learn if only they were given the proper chance."

He could see the sparks in her eyes as her imagination caught fire.

"Oh, Brandon, wouldn't that be wonderful?" she said, then sighed. "But it's impossible."

"Why?"

"Money, for one thing."

"I have more than I could ever spend," he said, thinking of what such a school might have meant for a boy like Sammy. "I think a school might be the kind of legacy a man could be proud of. Lacey's looking for projects, too. She's talked Kevin and me into a Halloran Foundation. It's a grand idea. I can't imagine why I never thought of it myself. Come on, Lizzy. What do you say? You provide the brainpower and I'll provide the cash."

She reached over and patted his hand. "You are a dear for even thinking of such a generous offer, but no. It's impossible. You're being impulsive and I'm far too old to begin such a massive endeavor."

"No," he said fiercely. "The idea may be impulsive, but it's a sound one. And don't ever say you're too old, Lizzy. Thinking like that will make you old before your time. I've found that looking forward to a new challenge each and every day keeps a man alive. Promise me you'll think about it."

She hesitated, then said, "I suppose I could promise that much, at least."

He nodded in satisfaction as he found a parking space near the marketplace. "That's good. Now let's find some good old-fashioned junk food and indulge ourselves without a thought for cholesterol or fiber."

That lively spark was back in her eyes when she met his gaze. "Hot dogs with mustard and relish, French fries—"

"And a hot-fudge sundae for dessert," he said, completing the menu they'd shared more than once in those long-ago days. He'd wanted to eat his fill of those American favorites before being relegated to the dismal rations of wartime England. "Do you have any idea how I missed those things while I was gone?"

"I don't see how you could. It's a wonder you didn't make yourself sick, you ate so many hot dogs."

Brandon couldn't help chuckling at the memory. Lizzy was laughing right along with him, her lips parted, her eyes alight with shared amusement. Suddenly he couldn't resist leaning toward her and touching his lips to hers, catching the sound of her laughter. The kiss lasted no longer than the melting touch of a snowflake, but it stirred the embers of a fire that had once burned more brightly than anything either of them had ever known.

Shaken to discover that those old feelings could be rekindled so easily and with such a sense of inevitability, Brandon drew back slowly.

"Ah, Lizzy," he said softly. "You'll never know how happy I am that you decided to come to Boston."

Her voice just as quiet and serious as his, she said, "I think maybe I do."

The silence that fell then was alive with a new, exciting tension. Brandon wondered how he'd gone so long without such feelings. Had he simply forgotten what it was like to experience this edge-of-a-precipice sensation? Now that he'd rediscovered it, would he ever be able to go back to the dull loneliness he'd almost fooled himself into thinking was bearable?

Since such questions couldn't be answered in the blink of an eye, he finally broke the tension by catching Lizzy's hand in his. "Come on, gal. Let's go see how much trouble we can get ourselves into."

Aside from their culinary indulgences, though, they left the marketplace by mid-afternoon with no more than a handful of souvenirs for Elizabeth to take back to her family in California. There'd been a dozen things he'd been tempted to buy for her, but she'd firmly declined each and every one.

"It's far too soon to call it quits for the day," Brandon said when they got back to the car. "How do you feel about visiting the public gardens? If I remember correctly, the swan boats are back in the water."

"Oh, what fun!" she said.

The ride aboard the paddleboats was over far too quickly for either of them, so they took a second ride and then a third until the boat's captain began regarding them with amusement.

When they finally left the boat, he winked at Brandon. "Now you folks have a nice afternoon."

"We already have," Lizzy told him. "This has been a wonderful chance to put our feet up."

"And I thought it was holding my hand you enjoyed most," Brandon said, bringing a blush into Lizzy's cheeks.

As they walked away, she said to Brandon, "What must that man think of us?"

"That we're very lucky," he told her as they walked lazily along the paths. "And we are lucky, Lizzy. We're more fortunate than most people. We've found each other, not once, but twice. Now how shall we spend our evening?"

"I intend to spend mine with my feet propped up and a cup of tea from room service. I haven't walked so much in ages."

"What a waste of time that would be. I know a wonderful neighborhood Italian restaurant with red-checked tablecloths and candles stuck in old Chianti bottles. The owner makes an absolutely decadent lasagna."

"Another time," she said firmly.

He could see that there would be no swaying her on this. He hid his disappointment and said only, "If you promise that you'll give me time enough to show you all my favorite places, I won't press about tonight." He grinned. "You know how persuasive I can be when I set my mind to it."

"Oh, yes," she said. "I do know that."

"Then you promise?"

"I promise to think about it," she agreed.

Content that that was the best he could manage, he drove back to her hotel and helped her inside with all of her packages.

"It was a splendid day," Elizabeth said, squeezing Brandon's hands as they stood in the lobby. "I really can't remember when I've had such fun."

"Are you sure you don't want a cocktail at least?"

"Absolutely. You've worn me out. I'm just going to pick up my messages and go upstairs and get out of these shoes."

"You should have let me buy you those high-top sneakers we saw," he teased.

"If I went home with high-top, hot-pink sneakers, my daughters would have me committed."

"Wouldn't hurt to shake them up once in a while. That's what I've found with Kevin and my grandson. Whenever they get to thinking I'm stodgy, I do something outrageous. I want you to meet them while you're here."

"Am I the outrageousness you mean to stir them up with this time?"

"I suppose they might see it that way. Seriously, Lizzy, shall I plan a family dinner?"

Elizabeth tried to imagine such a scene. One part of her wanted desperately to meet his son and the lovely daughter-in-law Brandon had described so clearly. She felt an inexplicable bond with his zany granddaughter-in-law. And she suspected Jason would be a heart-breaking reminder of the way Brandon had looked when they had met. Could she possibly meet them all and not regret the past that had made them another woman's family, instead of her own?

"I think not," she said a little sadly.

Brandon's gaze narrowed as he studied her. "Why? What's wrong, Lizzy?"

"Nothing's wrong, Brandon. I just don't see any point to it."

"Does there have to be a point to having dinner with an old friend's family?"

"Are you saying this would be no more than a casual get-together?"

"Did you want it to be more?"

With his gaze burning into her, she shook her head and put a decisive note into her voice. "No. I made my intentions clear, Brandon. There's no going back for us."

Finally he shrugged. "Whatever you like. We'll discuss it again tomorrow. What time shall I pick you up? Or would you rather come to the house for breakfast? I could send the car."

The idea of sitting across a breakfast table from Brandon held a provocative appeal she couldn't resist. "I would love to come for breakfast."

"Wonderful. I'll have Mrs. Farnsworth make her famous apple pancakes."

"A bowl of cereal and some fruit would do. She needn't go to any trouble for me."

"Apple pancakes are her specialty. She would be disappointed if you didn't try them. Besides, she never makes them just for me and I love them."

"Then, by all means, the apple pancakes. About eight-thirty?"

"I'll send the car at eight," he said.

Secretly delighted by his impatience, she repeated firmly, "Eight-thirty. You have to remember I'm still on California time. That's practically the middle of the night for me."

"I seem to recall nights when we sat up until dawn."

"And I seem to recall that at that age we never required eight hours of sleep. We could run on pure adrenaline."

"Don't you go trying to make yourself sound old. I saw the way your foot tapped when we heard that music earlier at the marketplace. I'm taking you dancing one of these nights."

She chuckled at the feigned ferocity in his expression. "Is that an invitation or a threat, Brandon Halloran?"

"Whichever works," he said, reaching out with surprisingly unsteady fingers to trace the curve of her cheek. He brushed gently at the wisps of hair that feathered around her face. "I can't get over the way you look with your hair like this. I couldn't imagine you ever being more beautiful than you were when we met, but you are, Lizzy. Like a rare wine, you've aged with dignity."

"And you're a sentimental old fool," she said gently, but she couldn't deny the sweet rush of pleasure that sped through her. She placed her hand over his and before she could think about it, brought his hand to her lips and pressed a kiss to his knuckles. "Good night, Brandon."

He leaned forward and touched his lips to her forehead. "Night, Lizzy. I can't wait till morning."

He turned then and strolled away, his step jaunty, his shoulders squared. She couldn't be sure, but it sounded as if he might be whistling the chorus of that old Glenn Miller song they'd called their own.

Chapter Six

When he'd encouraged Elizabeth to come for breakfast, Brandon hadn't stopped to consider that the next day was Saturday. On Saturdays he could never count on not having the morning interrupted. More often than not, Jason and Dana dropped by with Sammy in tow. Occasionally even Kevin and Lacey turned up, lured by Mrs. Farnsworth's delectable apple pancakes.

Perhaps, subliminally, he had hoped the whole clan would drop in, taking matters out of his hands. It would give him a chance to introduce Elizabeth despite her uncertainty about the wisdom of such a meeting. He might have mixed feelings about subjecting her to their scrutiny, but his desire to hasten a relationship between them far outweighed any reservations he might have.

Sure enough, no sooner had he seated Lizzy at the dining room table and served her a cup of coffee than the front door banged open and Dana's brother came barreling in.

"Hey, Grandpa Brandon, are you up yet?" Sammy yelled loudly enough to wake the dead.

"If I weren't, I would be now," he observed mildly as Sammy rounded the corner into the dining room.

Looking nonplussed, the teenager screeched to a halt at the sight of Brandon's company.

Elizabeth looked equally startled by the sight of the lanky young man with his hair moussed into spikes, his jeans frayed and a T-shirt that was emblazoned with the perfectly horrid bloodred design of some new music group. Actually it was one of his more reserved outfits.

"Sorry," Sammy said, his gaze shifting from Elizabeth to Brandon and back again. A knowing grin spread across his face. "I guess we should have called, huh?"

"It wouldn't hurt to observe the amenities," Brandon confirmed.

Sammy regarded him blankly. "The what?"

"You should have called. How'd you get here?" he asked suspiciously, expecting the worst.

His answer came in the form of the front door opening again. "Hey, Granddad," Jason called from the foyer. "We just came by to drop off your car and see how you're..." His voice trailed off as he reached the dining room and spotted Brandon's guest. "I guess you're doing fine."

"I *was*," Brandon said with an air of resignation. Suddenly he wished he'd relied more on caution, than impatience. "Lizzy, my grandson Jason. And our first intruder with the lousy manners is his young brother-in-law, Sammy Roberts. This is Elizabeth Newton."

"Hey," Sammy said, already seated at the table. "Jason, you were right. Mrs. Farnsworth is making those funny pancakes."

Brandon glanced at Lizzy's frozen expression and sighed. "I don't suppose you're in a hurry?" he inquired of the interlopers. The broad hint fell on deaf ears.

"Nope," Jason confirmed entirely too cheerfully. "We have all morning. Right, Sammy?"

"Yep. All morning."

"How lovely," Brandon said dryly. "Before you sit down, stick your head into the kitchen and tell Mrs. Farnsworth there will be four of us for breakfast, unless of course Dana is planning to wander in at any moment, as well."

"Nope. I think you can safely count her out. She's home practicing her breathing," Jason said.

"I thought you were supposed to help with that."

"She says I make her nervous."

"Probably because you hyperventilate," Brandon said critically. "I told you I'd be happy to assist. I have much more experience at remaining calm under trying circumstances." He purposely neglected to add that this morning was rapidly turning into a perfect example.

"Granddad, as much as I adore you, you are *not* going to take my place in the delivery room," Jason said patiently.

"You and me can pace the halls together," Sammy offered as a consolation. "You gotta bring the cigars, though. Dana says if she catches me with one, she'll tan my hide."

Brandon glanced over to see if Elizabeth was beginning to take all this with the sort of aplomb she'd been capable of years ago. Given her protest the day before when he'd suggested a family dinner, he thought she was doing rather well. He couldn't quite identify her expression, though. Astonishment and dismay seemed to have given way to fascination. In fact her gaze was fastened on Jason as if just looking at him carried her back in time.

"Lizzy?" Brandon said softly.

She blinked and turned to him. "The resemblance is remarkable," she murmured. Then as if she thought she'd said too much, she added quickly, "Do you really want to be in the delivery room?"

Jason, apparently oblivious to the meaning of her first remark, seized the second and grinned at her astonishment. "He's afraid the rest of us will botch it."

Brandon considered offering a rebuttal, but decided that Jason was pretty close to the truth. He wanted nothing to go wrong with the birth of his first great-grandchild. He hated trusting anything so critical to other people.

Of course, he hadn't been anywhere near the delivery room when Kevin was born. Even if the hospital had allowed it back then, Grace would never have permitted it. She would have thought it unseemly for him to witness her in the throes of labor. He was downright envious of all these young husbands today who got to share in one of God's own miracles.

"So, how do you and Granddad know each other?" Jason asked Elizabeth.

Jason's tone might be all innocent curiosity, Brandon thought worriedly, but that gleam in his eye was pure mischief. He had a hunch Dana had encouraged this visit by providing a few details about their encounter the previous morning. Elizabeth must not have caught that spark of devilment or she'd have been more cautious with her answer.

"We're old friends," she said, opening the door to a Pandora's box of speculation.

"You live here in Boston?"

"No, California."

"Ah, I see," Jason murmured, looking infinitely pleased.

"What are you grinning at?" Brandon grumbled.

"The flowers," Jason said.

"What flowers?" Sammy asked.

"Grandpa Brandon has been sending a lot of flowers to California lately."

"Why?" Sammy glanced at Elizabeth. "Oh, yeah, I get it. I guess that's why there are roses on the table, too, huh? There never have been before."

Sammy looked as if he were on the verge of making some even more outlandish remark. Brandon grasped at the first conversational gambit he could think of to deter him. "Sammy, if you're finished with breakfast, perhaps you'd like to go play some of those infernal video games you insisted I buy."

"Nah, I think I'll stick around for another pancake. Besides, it sounds like this could get interesting."

"I assure you it will not get to be anything close to interesting by your standards," Brandon commented. "Go play video games. Mrs. Farnsworth will be happy to bring your pancake to you in the library."

Sammy had no sooner shoved his chair back and departed than Jason said cheerfully, "So, Mrs. Newton, what exactly brings you to Boston?"

Color suddenly flooded Lizzy's cheeks as she realized how neatly Jason was backing her into the proverbial corner. Brandon tried to rescue her. "She's just here to do a little sight-seeing."

"That's right," she confirmed hurriedly. "It's been ages since I've seen all the sights in Boston."

"And how long has it been since you two last saw each other?"

She glanced desperately toward Brandon, then said, "Nearly fifty years."

"My goodness," Jason said, looking a little taken aback himself. "You've kept in touch, though, right?"

"No."

"Jason!" Brandon said with a soft warning note in his voice. "You're being impertinent."

His grandson ignored him. A grin slowly broke across his face. "This gets better and better, like one of those newspaper features you see on Valentine's day. Are you saying you'd lost touch? How'd you find each other again?"

Brandon watched as Elizabeth grew increasingly flustered. Finally he snapped, "Jason! This is none of your business."

His blasted grandson laughed at that.

"I know," he said delightedly.

"Jason Halloran, I am warning you," Brandon blustered. "If you don't behave, I'll..." Words failed him.

"You'll what, Granddad? Cut me out of the will?" He turned to Elizabeth. "I apologize if I've made you uncomfortable, but Granddad has this habit of meddling in our lives. He thinks it's his God-given right."

Apparently no longer caught off guard, the take-any-dare Lizzy of old suddenly emerged and seized the opportunity Jason had just handed her. She grinned, a genuine spark of devilment flaring in her eyes. Brandon didn't trust that spark one little bit.

"I can see how that would be taxing," she said. "Perhaps it would help if I offered a little ammunition. I gather he hasn't mentioned how he tracked me down?"

Brandon regarded her indignantly. *"Et tu, Brute?"*

She smiled and delivered the knockout punch without so much as an instant's caution. "He hired a detective. Isn't that like something right out of a movie?"

"Oh, Lord," Brandon moaned. "I will never, ever hear the end of this."

"No," Jason said, "you won't. I'm just sorry I didn't know about Mrs. Newton sooner. I might have hired that detective myself and brought her here to surprise you. I do love surprises, don't you, Mrs. Newton?"

"Absolutely," she said.

"If the two of you are going to be in cahoots," Brandon grumbled, "I might as well go play those video games with Sammy."

"Go ahead, Granddad. I'm sure Mrs. Newton and I could find plenty to talk about."

"Yes," she agreed. "I suspect we could. You'd probably find a talk about old times fascinating. My youngest granddaughter surely does."

Brandon regarded the two of them irritably. "On second thought, I guess I'll sit right here and watch out for my interests. I might remind you, though, Jason, that if it weren't for my meddling, you and Dana would probably not be married."

Jason instantly sobered. "You're right. I do owe you one for that."

"I should say so," Brandon said.

"Perhaps now would be the time to return the favor," Jason said slyly.

Brandon's gaze narrowed. "You could find yourself peddling pencils on street corners, if you're not careful," he warned grimly. "Now could we please talk about something else? Or perhaps you and Sammy would like to run along so Lizzy and I can get started on another day of sight-seeing."

"Where did you go yesterday?" Jason asked.

"The public gardens," Elizabeth said.

"Rode in one of the swan boats, I suppose?"

"Of course," she said, giving Jason a conspiratorial wink. "Three times. Your grandfather's quite the romantic, especially on these summer-like days. That's when we met, you know. The summer of 1942. He was about to ship out for England. He swept me off my feet.''

''Oh, really,'' Jason said, shooting his grandfather a speculative look.

Brandon glared at both of them. ''Lizzy, if I'd known what trouble you were going to give me, I would have insisted on coming to California. You just wait. I'll get even when I meet up with those daughters of yours. You won't know a moment's peace when I'm through.''

Instantly her amusement vanished. The change was so subtle that at first Brandon thought maybe he'd imagined it, but when she remained too silent for too long, he shot her a look of genuine concern.

''Lizzy?'' he said softly. ''You okay?''

''Fine, Brandon.''

She'd said the words, but there was no spunk behind them. Even Jason seemed puzzled by the change that had come over her.

''I'd better get Sammy and go,'' he said. ''Dana will be wondering what happened to us. We told her we were going out for juice.''

''And then you sneaked over here to spy on me,'' Brandon said. ''Now that's one I can hold over you.''

''Don't get your hopes up, Granddad. I suspect Sammy will spill the beans before you ever get a chance to.'' He turned to Elizabeth and clasped her hand in his. "It was nice meeting you, Mrs. Newton. I hope you'll be around for a while."

Lizzy's smile was genuine. "Meeting you and Sammy was my pleasure."

Jason leaned close and whispered something that made her laugh. Only after his grandson had gone did Brandon ask, "What was that he said to you?"

"He suggested I give you a run for your money."

"I like the sound of that," he said. "Lizzy, why did you go so quiet a few minutes ago? When I mentioned California, you clammed right up. You did the same thing the first time we talked on the phone."

He could tell how flustered she was by the way she was twisting her napkin and by the way her gaze evaded his. He'd never known the Lizzy of old to be at a loss for words. One of these days he'd have to accept that there were bound to be some changes over all this time, but at the moment he found this change particularly puzzling.

"I just can't see you being comfortable in my world," she said finally in a desperate tone that had him guessing that she was improvising.

"I never heard such a crazy idea," he protested, startled that she could even think such a thing. "You and I were comfortable from the first minute we met. Nothing's changed, Lizzy. Nothing. Why, when you stepped out of my car night before last, I felt all those years just slip away. I could be comfortable anywhere with you."

"You're wrong if you think there haven't been changes," she said adamantly. "A lot of time's gone by since then. We aren't the same people."

"We are in all the ways that count," he insisted just as stubbornly.

"Don't press, Brandon. Not on this."

Troubled by the expression of genuine dismay on her face, he reluctantly nodded his agreement. Then he spent the rest of the day wondering if he'd made a terrible mistake not forcing her to explain why she was more skittish around him now than when she'd been an innocent young virgin.

Elizabeth couldn't get to sleep, despite another long day of visiting Brandon's favorite haunts all over Boston. She was still deeply troubled by the conversation they'd had that morning.

Brandon had seen right through her. He'd guessed that she didn't want him in California, which was why she had to go back before he could get any notions about coming with her. Unfortunately he already seemed to have some pretty strong ideas about the future—crazy ideas that a man his age shouldn't be thinking. Even if she could entirely forget old hurts, too many things stood in their way. Things she could never explain. She had to put his crazy ideas out of his mind.

Because she didn't want to get caught up in the same fantasy, Elizabeth tried reading a paperback she'd picked up at the airport, but it was no better now than it had been when she'd tried to read it on the plane. She used the remote to switch on the television, skipped through the channels and couldn't find even an old movie to hold her interest.

"Face it, Elizabeth," she muttered under her breath, "you're not going to sleep until you deal with what's going on between you and Brandon."

He seemed to have this ridiculous notion that they could pick up right where they'd left off, as if they were a couple of kids. Why couldn't he see that the years had shaped them into very different people?

He was a business tycoon, for heaven's sake. She was a semiretired school teacher. He had traveled all over the world. Since moving to California, she'd rarely left—except for one incredible trip to Hawaii that the kids had given to her and David for their anniversary the year before he'd died. Brandon had a custom-tailored wardrobe, a six-bedroom mansion, a house-keeper and a chauffeur. Her clothes were off the rack, she owned a five-room house and did all of her own cooking, cleaning and driving. Years ago maybe none of that would have mattered. Today it seemed insurmountable.

It wasn't that she was insecure. Far from it, in fact. She knew her own worth, but she could take a realistic measure of that and see that it didn't stack up to be the right woman for a confident, sophisticated man like Brandon Halloran.

Of course, those were only excuses, she admitted reluctantly. There were far more pressing reasons why they couldn't have a future together, but she couldn't even bring herself to think about those.

Elizabeth was questioning whether it was even wise to remain in Boston for the duration of her promised visit, when the phone rang. It was nearly 1:00 a.m., but just before 10:00 p.m. in California.

Almost glad of the late-hour interruption, she grabbed the phone on the second ring, only to be greeted by Kate's exasperated "Mother!"

"Hello, darling. I see you've tracked me down."

"I wouldn't have had to do any tracking, if you'd seen fit to tell me you were going away," she declared, clearly annoyed.

"Sweetheart, you've been away on business for the past two weeks. How was I supposed to tell you?"

"The office would have told you how to find me."

"And if it had been an emergency, I might have called," she said reasonably. "I saw no reason to do so just because I was flying to Boston for a few days."

"Why on earth would you go to Boston after all this time? You haven't been back there in years."

"Decades, actually."

"So, why did you decide to go on the spur of the moment?"

Since Ellen had obviously reported the trip to Kate, Elizabeth wished her older daughter had also given Kate all the explanations. Maybe then Elizabeth would be feeling less defensive.

"An old friend called and invited me."

Kate paused at that. "I didn't know you kept in touch with anyone back there."

"Dear, you haven't exactly kept tabs on my correspondence, have you? Nor do you tell me about all of your trips and contracts," she pointed out.

"Then you have been in touch with this person?"

"Kate, darling, I really think you're making much too much of this. I'll be home in a few days and I'll tell you all about it. In the meantime, why don't you tell me how your business trip went? Did you win that divorce case for your client in Palm Springs?"

Momentarily distracted just as Elizabeth had hoped she would be, Kate said, "We're still haggling over the settlement. The man has become a multimillionaire, thanks to his wife's investment savvy. He wants to hold her to a prenuptial agreement written in the dark ages."

"I really do wish you'd gotten into some other aspect of law," Elizabeth told her. "I think you've developed a very jaded view of marriage by handling all these high-profile, nasty divorce cases."

"Mother, I do not care to discuss my views on marriage and romance. We both know that I think they're highly overrated."

Elizabeth sighed wearily. "I can't imagine how you could come to that view after growing up around your father and me."

"Believe me, you were the exceptions, not the rule. Don't blame yourself. You set a wonderful example. I've just seen too many of my friends and my clients get royally screwed once the romance dies."

"I think you'd change your mind, if you ever met the right young man," Elizabeth countered. "How is that attractive new partner in your firm? Lance Hopkins, wasn't it? I believe you mentioned he's single."

"You and Ellen," Kate grumbled. "You're both far too romantic for your own good. I never mentioned that Lance Hopkins is single and you know it. Ellen concocted some excuse to pry the information out of my secretary. Now stop trying to change the subject. I want to know whom you're visiting and when you expect to be back home."

"I'll be back in a few days. We'll talk about it then," she replied firmly.

"Mother, are you there with some man?" Kate asked suspiciously.

"If I were, it would be none of your business. You worry about your social life, young lady, and let me take care of my own."

"Mother," Kate protested, but Elizabeth was already lowering the phone back into its cradle.

Okay, maybe hanging up was the cowardly way out. But it was one thing to sit in this hotel room so far from home wondering if she was crazy for coming to Boston, crazier yet for not running away as fast as she could. It would be quite another to have her levelheaded daughter confirm it.

Chapter Seven

Brandon was up at the crack of dawn, anxious to get the day under way, more optimistic than he had been in years. Since Mrs. Farnsworth was off on Sundays, he made his own coffee, then glanced through the first section of the paper. Not one paragraph, not even one headline he read registered. He turned the pages mechanically, thinking only of how light his heart had become since Lizzy had come back into his life.

Unfortunately the cursory study of the newspaper didn't waste nearly enough time. It was barely seven. He read the business section, then the sports section, and killed another half hour. He glanced at his watch impatiently, muttered a curse and picked up the phone.

Elizabeth's sleepy greeting set his blood to racing. How many times had he dreamed of waking beside her and hearing just such an innocently seductive purr in her voice? A half-dozen times in the past few weeks alone. Multiply that by years, when the memory of her crept in when he least expected it.

"Good morning," he said briskly. "I'm sorry if I woke you."

"You don't sound sorry," she said, laughter lacing through her voice. "What are you doing calling so early?"

"I didn't want to waste a minute of this beautiful day. How about coming to church with me, then going for a drive to see all the spring flowers in bloom? I know a wonderful old inn that would be the perfect place for lunch. If I play my cards right, I might even be able to borrow Dana's car again."

"It sounds lovely."

"Can you be ready in an hour? The service I had in mind is at nine."

"I'll be ready," she promised.

Brandon tried not to feel guilty as he rushed through his shower and dressed in a dark blue suit, a pale blue shirt and a silk tie—all made of Halloran fabrics. Maybe he should have mentioned that Lacey and Kevin were likely to be at the services.

Then again, he consoled himself, he wasn't absolutely certain they would be. They might even be out on

Cape Cod, where they were spending more and more time since Kevin's last heart attack. No need getting Elizabeth all worked up over nothing. She'd handled the impromptu meeting with Jason and Sammy blithely enough. In the long run maybe it was better to spring things on her, so she didn't have time to fret and find a dozen excuses for saying no.

An hour later, with Lizzy by his side, he was pulling into the church parking lot.

"What a beautiful old church," Elizabeth said of the plain white structure with its intricately designed stained glass windows and towering steeple.

"Wait until you see it inside," he told her, imagining it through her eyes. "The light filters through all that glass and creates a rainbow of colors."

Just then the bell began to chime, its resonance pure and strong as it filled the air.

"Let's get inside before the processional starts," he said.

He led the way to a pew halfway up the wide, carpeted aisle just as the first hymn began. He found the song in the hymnal and offered it to Elizabeth, but she was already singing in her clear soprano. Even so, in a gesture he remembered vividly from another long-ago Sunday, she placed her hand next to his so they could share.

As he stood next to her, fingers barely touching, and listened to the verses of the hymn, he realized that he had never felt so blessed or so joyous. Unexpected contentment stole through him. Finding his precious Elizabeth again must have been God's work.

She glanced up then and smiled, her face radiant. "You're not singing," she whispered.

He looked down, reminding himself of the familiar words, and then he too sang along with the congregation, his bass joining her sweet voice to soar above all the rest.

Brandon was oblivious to the rest of the service. Though he normally found the minister's sermons to be lively and meaningful, today he was far too conscious of the woman seated next to him. He couldn't stop himself from thinking that if all had gone the way he'd wanted years ago, she would have walked down this very aisle to become his bride.

As the service ended, he took Elizabeth's elbow and steered her through the crowd, murmuring greetings to friends, many of whom he'd known his whole life. He liked the continuity of that, just as he liked thinking that a relationship he'd once cherished was just as strong decades later.

But only for him, he conceded reluctantly. He knew deep down he had yet to win Lizzy over to that way of thinking.

Outside they lingered to chat with the minister. Elizabeth praised the sermon, but Brandon was forced to mutter some innocuous statement because he couldn't recall the topic, much less anything his old friend had said.

He was just about to beat a hasty retreat, when he heard Kevin's voice behind him.

"Dad, I didn't see you earlier. You must have been late."

"We got here just before the processional," he said, turning to face his son and Lacey. He kissed his daughter-in-law. "Good morning, you two. I thought maybe you'd be out at the Cape this weekend."

"Thought or hoped?" Lacey asked, with a pointed glance at Elizabeth. "I understand you have company. Hello, I'm Lacey Halloran and this is Kevin."

"This is Elizabeth Newton," Brandon said, watching Lizzy's face for some indication of her reaction to this chance meeting with his son and daughter-in-law. Judging from the glance she shot his way, he was going to hear about this encounter later. She might forgive one meeting as chance, but two in a row were bound to look suspicious in her eyes.

"It's a pleasure to meet you both," she said graciously. "Brandon has told me quite a lot about you."

Kevin scowled. "Funny, he hasn't told us a thing about you. Have you been keeping secrets, Dad?"

His tone was teasing, but there was an underlying thread of dismay that Brandon caught even if no one else did. Fortunately Lacey had a knack for putting people at ease and she was already chatting a mile a minute with Lizzy, asking about California, her family, her teaching.

"That reminds me," Brandon said. "Lizzy and I were talking about the need for a school that could cater to youngsters like Sammy, children who are bright enough, but need an extra boost if they're to succeed. You two should talk about it."

"What a wonderful idea!" Lacey exclaimed and began asking Lizzy questions in a voice filled with enthusiasm.

Brandon listened to them in satisfaction. Two of a kind, he thought complacently, just as Kevin pulled him aside.

"Who is this woman?" his son demanded.

Brandon stared at him, startled by his thoroughly disgruntled tone. "You say that as if she's got a big scarlet A pinned to her dress. What on earth's the matter with you?"

"I don't like it, Dad. You're quite a catch for any woman. I don't want to see you taken advantage of. Jason mentioned you hadn't seen this woman for almost fifty years. Out of the blue, she turns up again, now that Mother's dead. Quite a coincidence, wouldn't you say?"

Brandon felt his temper starting to boil. "Son, that is enough! Elizabeth is a fine woman. If you'd done a little checking instead of flinging around slanderous opinions, you would have known that I went after her, not the other way around."

The visible tension in Kevin's shoulders eased some at that explanation. "Okay, maybe I misunderstood, but a man in your position needs to be careful, Dad. You're vulnerable with Mother gone. It would be easy enough for some gold digger to come along and take advantage of you. There are a dozen women right here in town, women you've known forever, who would be happy to share your life with you, if you feel the need for companionship."

"You make it sound about as simple as choosing a puppy and training it to fetch my slippers," Brandon grumbled. "I suppose I should have expected this. It's more retaliation for all my meddling over the years. Kevin, don't you think I have sense enough to spot a devious, conniving woman?"

"Frankly, no. You always did have a romantic streak. You'd imagine you were in love, no matter what the circumstances were."

"You let me worry about my imagination. Unfortunately, I suspect what you're really worried about is your inheritance," he said with an undeniable edge of sarcasm.

Kevin couldn't have looked more shocked if Brandon had accused him of embezzling. "Dad, you know that's not true."

Brandon sighed heavily. "I'm sorry. You're right. I know you're just thinking of me, but believe me, son, I know what I'm doing."

"Is this relationship serious?"

"At the moment, let's just say it's a serious flirtation. I don't think Lizzy would stand for anything more." He glanced at her and his expression softened. "I do believe, though, that I will do anything in my power to change that."

"Just go slowly, Dad. Promise me that."

"Son, at my age, there's not time enough left to go slow. I plan to grab whatever happiness I can. Don't begrudge me that." He moved back to Lizzy's side. "You ready for that drive in the country?"

"Indeed, I am," she said, smiling up at him.

"Have a good time, you two," Lacey said.

"We intend to," Brandon replied, hoping that Lizzy hadn't noticed Kevin's failure to join in Lacey's best wishes.

When they were alone in the car, though, she turned a troubled gaze toward him. "Kevin's unhappy about my being here, isn't he?"

"I wouldn't say unhappy."

"What would you say?"

"Concerned."

She sighed. "Isn't it amazing that we can live an entire lifetime, raise families, hold jobs, suffer devastating losses, and our kids still think we haven't got the brains the good Lord gave a duck?''

He chuckled. "You've been getting the third degree, too?"

"Only from my youngest. She called last night to fuss at me for not notifying her that I planned this trip. I tried to point out that she almost never tells me when or where she's going on a business trip, but she didn't quite get the similarity."

"Are you sure it's the same thing?" he asked. "Or did you make a point of *not* telling her, because you knew she wouldn't approve?"

"I could ask you the same thing. Seems to me like I was a big surprise to everyone in your family."

"Touché," he said. He glanced over at her. "Let's make a pact that we will not allow family interference to get in the way of you and me having the time of our lives."

"If we had a little champagne, I'd drink a toast to that," she agreed, reaching for his hand. "Sometimes it seems you know exactly what's on my mind."

"Because we're more alike than you want to admit. Now let's forget all our cares and take in this beautiful scenery. I'm sorry Dana wasn't at church so we could borrow her car, but spring's putting on a show for us just the same. And I, for one, don't want to miss it."

Elizabeth released his hand and looked out the window at the budding trees about to burst forth with dogwood blossoms. Bright yellow forsythia spilled over split-rail fences. Purple and white lilac scented the air.

"I'd forgotten how beautiful it is here in the spring. We have a change of seasons in California, but it's not nearly as dramatic. Everything is bright and bold there, almost the whole year around. Here you go from dreary grays and stark browns to pastels. I guess it's sort of like comparing the soft colors chosen by Monet to the brilliant palette of Van Gogh or Gauguin."

"With that kind of poetry in your soul, you'll love the place we're going for lunch."

"Tell me," she urged, her voice laced with curiosity. She'd always wished for the time to discover romantic hideaways. David had been content with bland, ordinary restaurants and hotel chains.

"I'm not spoiling the surprise. You'll have to see what I mean when we get there."

They reached the inn a half hour later, a huge old clapboard house painted white and trimmed with black shutters. A weather vane on the roof twirled in the breeze. Though it was lovely, it wasn't until they were inside that Elizabeth could see what Brandon had meant.

The entire back of the house had been redone with French doors that were glass from floor to ceiling. Beyond the doors was a patio that had not yet been opened. It was edged with honeysuckle tumbling over a white picket fence. The scent was sweeter than any air she'd breathed in years.

Beyond the inn's yard, the hillside spilled into a valley that was brilliant with thousands of tulips, daffodils and the bright green of new grass. If they'd taken a patch of the Netherlands in springtime and transported it to this site, it could not have been more beautiful.

Elizabeth drew in a deep breath of the air coming through the open doors and smiled in delight. She looked over and caught Brandon's gaze pinned on her.

"You like it?" he asked anxiously.

"I've never been anywhere like it. Thank you for bringing me."

"I didn't bring you just because of the picturesque view. The food is marvelous here, too."

Everyone seemed to know Brandon well, from the hostess to the waitress to the owner, who stopped by to ensure that everything was to their liking.

"You must come here often," she said, realizing as she said it that she sounded oddly miffed.

"Once or twice a year," he said.

"Then you must tip very generously to warrant all the attention."

He grinned so broadly that she felt color flooding into her cheeks.

"Jealous, Lizzy?"

"No, I am not jealous," she snapped. Then because her tone made it sound more like a confirmation than a denial, she added, "It's certainly none of my business what you've done."

"That doesn't keep you from being a mite curious. Am I right?"

"Absolutely not!" she said with as much conviction as she could muster.

"I should let you go on trying to squirm off the hook, but I'll have mercy on you," he teased. "The owner is a client. Halloran provides all the custom fabrics for the place—from the draperies to the tablecloths to the seat cushions. Notice how they pick up the colors from outdoors and bring them inside."

"Oh, my," she said with delight as she caught the similarity. "Brandon, you amaze me. I should have guessed it was something like that."

"Instead of the wild, clandestine rendezvous you were imagining? Made me feel young again, just to know you thought me capable of such carrying on."

She gazed boldly into his eyes. "I don't know why I let you agitate me so. You always did love to tease me."

"Do you know why?"

Her breath seemed to go still. "Why?"

"Because you blushed so prettily. You still do, Lizzy."

He reached across the table and took her hand in his. She told herself she ought to draw away, but she couldn't bring herself to do it. His hand was warm and strong, a hand that could comfort or excite. She recalled that all too vividly despite the time that had passed. Foolish notions, she chided herself.

"Lizzy, do you know that not once in all the times I've been here did I bring another woman with me. Not even Grace."

"Why?"

"Because from the first time I saw it, it made me think of you."

Emotions crowded into her throat and tears stung her eyes. "Oh, Brandon, even if they're lies, you do say the most romantic things."

"It's not a lie," he said softly.

Whether it was or it wasn't, Elizabeth knew she didn't dare allow herself to fall for the tender web he was trying to spin around her heart.

It worried Brandon that Lizzy didn't trust him, especially when he knew he had only a short time to convince her of his sincerity. He wined and dined her. He wooed her with flowers. They shared quiet evenings at home and passionate arguments after movies. He tried to convince her to move into one of his guest rooms, but she was adamant about staying on at the hotel. He guessed that had as much to do with caution as it did with her sense of propriety.

In between, there were frantic calls from Kevin, who'd managed to dream up more questions about the running of Halloran Industries than he'd asked during the entire decade they'd worked together.

"Dad, can't you come in tomorrow? I think we should meet on the new contracts."

"You've been negotiating those contracts on your own for the past five years. You know I don't like to mess with that sort of detail. I was delighted to have you take it off my hands. Why should I want to change that now? Besides, Lizzy and I have plans."

"What plans?"

"None of your business," he said, because he was thinking of taking her to Maine for a nostalgic visit to the place they'd met. He intended to ask her tonight. "Kevin, I trust you to run Halloran Industries. I really do."

Kevin merely sighed in defeat and hung up.

That night Brandon took Lizzy dancing, though he stopped short of trying some of those fancy new steps that looked more suited to a bedroom than a public dance floor. In his day a man could have gotten his face slapped for some of those maneuvers. Damn, but they looked like fun, though.

Back at his place, he turned on the stereo and shot a glance at Lizzy, who'd ended the evening with her hair mussed and her cheeks flushed. He held out his arms.

*"What do you say? Want to try one of those new-fangled dances we saw tonight?"

"Get out of here, Brandon Halloran. We're too old."

Despite the protest, he saw the hint of curiosity in her eyes. "Not me. I'm feeling chipper as the day we met. Come on, Lizzy."

Breathless and laughing, they tried to imitate the intricate steps they'd seen earlier. As their bodies fit together intimately, the laughter suddenly died. Lizzy's startled gaze met his and years fell away.

Brandon touched his lips to hers with surprising caution, almost as if he feared a ladylike slap in response to a daring kiss. There was tenderness and longing in the tentative, velvet-soft kiss and the first breath of a passion that both had thought long over.

The flowery scent of Lizzy's perfume took Brandon back to the first time he'd dared to steal a kiss.

They had been in the garden behind the Halloran mansion, surrounded by the scent of spring and the gentle whisper of a breeze. He'd wanted Lizzy to meet his family, to see his home back then, too, but she'd been afraid. A little awestruck by the size of the house, she had come no farther than the garden before being overcome by second thoughts.

"They'll love you," he'd vowed, ignoring his own uncertainty to quiet hers.

"You can't just spring me on them days before you leave. They'll be certain you've taken leave of your senses."

"Do you love me?" he'd asked her quietly.

"Oh, yes." Her blue eyes sparkled like sapphires when she said it.

"Then that's all that matters." His mouth had covered hers, stilling her trembling lips.

There had been so much hope, so much sweet temptation in that kiss, he thought now. Was it any wonder she'd remained in his heart?

Brandon felt the stir of those same fragile emotions now, an echo that reverberated through him. They gave him the courage to speak his mind.

"Marry me, Lizzy," he said impulsively. "Don't let's make the same mistake twice."

Before the words were out of his mouth, he knew he should have waited, knew he should have settled for asking her to go back to Maine with him. There was no mistaking the flare of panic in her eyes, the way she trembled in his arms.

It was the sort of careless error that a man new to making deals might make, misjudging the opposition. Brandon cursed the arrogance that had misled him into thinking her misgivings were of no importance. Only a man totally blinded by love would not have seen that Lizzy wasn't ready to consider marriage.

Even so, he couldn't bring himself to withdraw the proposal, because more than anything he wanted her to say yes to it. But once the words were spoken, he could see that he'd made a terrible mistake. He'd underestimated her fears and exaggerated his claim on her heart.

Brandon's breath caught in his throat as he waited to see how much damage his impetuous proposal had done.

Chapter Eight

Elizabeth was caught off guard by Brandon's proposal now, just as she had been all those years back. For one crazy split second, she imagined saying yes. The word was on her lips as she thought how wonderful it would be to know that this strong, exciting man would spend the rest of his life at her side. She indulged herself in the fantasy that they would have a second chance at all the happiness they had lost.

As she struggled against her powerful desires, she was vibrantly aware of the ticking of an old grandfather clock, the whisper of branches against the library's glass doors. Everything seemed sharper and somehow dangerous as she flirted with Brandon's tempting offer.

There was no denying that it was romantic notions like that that had pulled her back to Boston in the first place. Yearnings, aroused by this compelling man, had kept her here beyond the scheduled end of the trip, but marriage? She had never really considered that an option because she knew it could never be. Never. Far too much was at risk. Once again she realized she would have to disappoint him—and, perhaps even more, herself.

She touched her fingers to his cheek. His skin was tanned and smooth with fine lines fanning out from the corners of his clear blue eyes. She recalled as vividly as if it had been only yesterday the first time she had dared to touch him intimately, the first time she had felt the sandpaper rasp of his unshaven face after they had lain in each other's arms for nearly an entire night of daring, blissful pleasure before parting discreetly before dawn. Then, as now, there had been as much sorrow as joy in her heart, knowing that their time together was drawing to a close.

"Oh, Brandon," she whispered now with a sigh as she tried to find the right words to make her refusal less painful for both of them. "You are such a dear, sweet man to ask. You almost sound as if you mean it."

"I *do* mean it," he said, radiating indignation. "I've never meant anything more. We're still good together, Lizzy. You can't deny that."

She tried to counter passionate impulsiveness with clear, cool reason. "No, I can't deny it. But you have your life here, and I have mine in California. This has been a wonderful time for us, but we can't go shaking things up so drastically. Not overnight like this. What would our families think?"

"That we've waited entirely too long," he said flatly.

How could he not see, she wondered, that what he said was only partly true? "Jason, perhaps. He's young and newly in love himself. Kevin is another story. Even you must recognize that. He sees me as an intruder, I'm sure."

"He'd see any woman who stepped into his mama's place that way. He'll come to terms with it. Besides, what does it matter what he thinks? If his attitude upsets you, I'll have another talk with him, explain the way it is with us. I won't allow him to make you feel uncomfortable."

Elizabeth laughed at his conviction that he could mold people's thoughts and deeds so easily. "Brandon, you might be able to force him into polite acceptance, but you can't very well change the way he feels. And isn't that what really counts?"

For an instant Brandon looked defeated, then his expression brightened. "I'll just remind him of how foolishly I behaved when I refused to recognize how important Lacey was to him. That'll make him see things more clearly."

"And what should I tell Kate? She'd be no happier to learn of our relationship than Kevin."

"Tell her that you love me," he said simply.

"I'm afraid she thinks that love is an illusion. At our age, she'd probably consider it insanity."

"Then we'll just have to show her otherwise. Lizzy, we can't let our children dictate our lives, any more than they allow us to interfere in theirs."

Elizabeth couldn't deny she was tempted, but she knew that part of the temptation for her—and for Brandon, whether he wanted to admit it or not—was based on memories that had managed to intertwine with the present. Those memories had given each moment of the past few days a bittersweet poignancy, had heightened every thrilling sensation. The tenderness, the laughter, the joy, how could they possibly be sure any of that was real?

Besides, she had meant what she'd said about their having separate lives. It was hard to get much farther apart than Boston and California. She couldn't bear the thought of not seeing her grandchildren.

And for all his stubborn denial, Brandon wouldn't like being separated from his family, either. Not that that was even a possibility. She would never have him in Los Angeles. The strain of it would kill her, though she couldn't tell him that. He'd guess in a minute the secret she was determined to keep to her death, no matter the cost to her personal happiness.

"What's the real reason, Lizzy?" he said as if he could see that she was dissembling. "You afraid to take a chance on a man my age?"

She scoffed at the ridiculous notion. "Brandon, you have more energy than men half your age. You'd still be running me ragged when we both turn eighty."

"I know that," he said with a twinkle in his eyes. "I just wondered if you did."

She raised her concerns about life-style and distance. But he shot each down promising to charter a jet if he had to to take her back and forth to California.

"So, you've assumed we'll settle here," she countered. "There you go again, making plans without a thought to what I might want."

"No, indeed. The only thing I care about is what you want. I'm just not sure you recognize what that is."

"Brandon, I do believe I know my own mind."

"Then say something that makes sense," he snapped impatiently.

His tone set her teeth on edge. "Just because you don't want to hear what I'm saying doesn't mean it doesn't make sense. Don't you think deciding where to live is critical for a couple our age?"

"I don't aim on settling anywhere. I'm thinking of seeing the world, getting myself out of Jason and Kevin's hair. Think about it, Lizzy. Have you been to Rome? Paris? Tahiti?''

Naturally Brandon would hit on an almost irresistible lure, she thought irritably. Just the sound of all those fascinating places thrilled her. They were rich with culture she'd only read about in books. She'd promised herself that one day she would see them all. Time was running out, but this wasn't the answer. They couldn't roam the world as if they were rootless, when the very opposite was true.

"Tahiti?" she inquired quizzically. "Isn't that a little exotic for the likes of us?"

"Why? I'll bet you still cut a fine figure in a bathing suit." His mood obviously improved, he winked when he said it, then sobered and added more seriously, "Besides, there are a lot of books I've been wanting to read. A month or two on the beach would help me to catch up." The twinkle came back. "Unless you'd prefer to lure me off to our room and have your way with me."

"Brandon!" Despite the stern disapproval in her tone, she couldn't banish the devilish quickening of her pulse. Brandon did have a way of saying the most outrageous things to shock her. Was she going to let silly fears and practicality stand in the way of happiness again? Perhaps a compromise was possible, a way to snag a few weeks or even months of pleasure.

"I've always wanted to run away to a tropical isle with a handsome stranger," she admitted, not even trying to hide the wistfulness.

Brandon's big, gentle hands cupped her cheeks. "We're hardly strangers, Lizzy. We've known each other our whole lives."

"But we've only been together less than a month, counting these past few days. Isn't that part of the appeal? We've never had time to recognize all the little idiosyncrasies that might drive us crazy."

"Is there anything important about me you don't know?"

"No," she had to admit. But there were things he didn't know about her, could never know. She could have a few more weeks, though. Just a few weeks of stolen happiness. They deserved that much.

"Let's just run away, Brandon," she coaxed. "There's no need for a ceremony. We needn't worry about shocking anyone in this day and age."

His hands fell away from her face. His eyes turned serious. "Do you think our children would be happier to see us having an affair than they would be seeing us married? I doubt it. Besides, I can't bear the thought of waking up some morning to discover you've vanished during the night. I want a real commitment this time, Lizzy. I won't settle for less."

"I can't give you that. I was never as brave or as strong as you, Brandon. I don't take risks."

"But there's no risk involved. Can't you see that? After all these years our feelings haven't changed. That should tell you how right they are. We've cherished them in our hearts. Not that either of us shortchanged the people we married." He tapped his chest. "But here, where it counts, we've never forgotten."

"Our feelings aren't the only ones that count anymore. We have families to consider."

"Dammit, Lizzy, you're thinking up excuses, not reasons."

"No," she said gently. "Your family is every bit as important to you as mine is to me. Neither of us could ever knowingly do something that would bring them unhappiness or pain."

"Lizzy, you're not making sense. How could our happiness cause them pain?"

She couldn't explain, no matter how badly she wanted to erase the confusion and hurt in his eyes.

"I'm sorry, Brandon," she whispered, fighting to hide the tears that threatened as she finalized the decision she should have made days earlier. "I'm going home in the morning. Alone."

He backed away from her then, and his expression turned colder than she'd ever seen it before. "I won't chase after you again, Lizzy."

She felt his anguish as deeply as her own. "I know," she said in a voice filled with regret. "Perhaps you should call a taxi to take me back to the hotel. We'll say our goodbyes here, just as we did the first time."

"No. I brought you here. I'll take you back," he said with stiff politeness.

"Really, it's not necessary."

"Yes," he said firmly. "It is."

The drive to the hotel was made in silence. It was colder by far in the car than it was outdoors. Elizabeth felt as if her heart had frozen inside her. She was certain she would never feel anything as magnificent as Brandon's caring again. She was trading love for peace of mind, and at the moment it seemed to be a lopsided exchange all the way around.

Brandon wondered how the devil things had gone so wrong again. Day after day, he'd seen the way Lizzy looked at him. He'd felt her pulse quicken at his touch, felt her flesh warm. Whatever the real explanation for her withdrawal, he knew he hadn't heard it yet. Not that she was lying. But she definitely wasn't telling him the whole truth.

He was a proud man, though. He wouldn't chase after her like some lovesick adolescent. If she couldn't be honest, if she couldn't trust him with the truth, then perhaps he'd been wrong all along about the depth of her feelings.

Perhaps it was just as well to discover now that there was no trust between them. They'd lost it over those damned letters decades back and nothing that had happened in the past few days had helped them to recapture it.

Maybe he'd fooled himself that what they'd once shared had been deeper and more meaningful than anything he'd experienced before or since. Maybe he'd simply been making a desperate, last grab for what had turned out to be no more than an illusion. Maybe love and marriage weren't even possible at his age. Perhaps he should be willing to settle for the fleeting companionship Lizzy offered. There were so damn many maybes, and so few solid answers.

Despite Lizzy's objections, Brandon turned the car over to the valet at the hotel and followed her inside. In front of the elevator he studied her and tried to convince himself that he'd been wrong about everything, but his heart ached with a real sense of loss. He might have tracked her down on impulse, but he'd kept her in Boston because she'd engaged his heart as no other woman ever had. He couldn't explain it, it just *was*— like the rising of the sun or the pull of the tides.

He brushed a wisp of hair back from her cheek and felt her tremble. His gaze caught hers and held them spellbound. Her lips parted on a soft sigh that could have been either pleasure or regret.

"I've spent the whole drive over here trying to convince myself that I'm wrong about us," he said finally, his knuckles grazing her soft cheek. "But I'd be a liar if I told you I believed it. There's a bond between us, Lizzy, one I can't deny. Can you?''

Her hand reached up and covered his. ''No,'' she said. ''I can't deny that.''

''Then why won't you marry me?''

''I can't,'' she said with stubborn finality, slipping away from his touch.

''I won't make it easy for you to walk away,'' he warned, just before he pulled her into his arms and brought his mouth down to cover hers.

Oblivious to everything except the woman melting in his embrace, Brandon plundered. It wasn't a kiss meant just to remind. It was meant to brand. It was a hot, hungry claiming of a kind he'd nearly forgotten until Lizzy had come back into his life.

Her scent, like that of spring rain and sweetest flowers, surrounded them. Her skin was petal soft, her lips moist and inviting after that first shocked instant when his tongue had invaded.

Despite its urgency, the kiss should have been the end of it, but it brought too many provocative memories, too many seductive images of another time, another place. His pulse bucked like a young man's, as it had on that single splendid night he and Lizzy had shared.

''Let me come to your room,'' he whispered in a voice husky with desire. ''If nothing else, let me hold you through this one last night.'' The words were an echo of a long-ago plea and he waited just as anxiously for her response. "Don't deny us that," he coaxed.

"Sometimes I wonder how I ever denied you anything," she said ruefully. She slid her hand into his. "One night, Brandon. I suppose there's no harm in grabbing that much happiness."

The elevator ride was the longest he'd ever taken. He couldn't stop looking at Lizzy, with her cheeks flushed with color and her eyes bright with anticipation. She looked every bit as beautiful tonight as she had as a girl, and he wanted her in his arms with the same aching urgency. Since Grace had died, he'd thought he would never again experience this fire in his blood, but it pulsed now with a demanding roar.

In Lizzy's room, the maid had turned down the expensive covers on the queen-size bed. A foil-wrapped candy was on each pillow. Light from the hall spilled in, until Brandon slowly shut the door behind them, leaving them in shadows.

He reached for the light, but Lizzy stayed his hand. "No," she whispered. "I want you to remember me the way I was, not the way I am now."

He touched her cheek in a gesture meant to reassure. "You will always be beautiful in my eyes. Time could never change that."

"Spoken like a true romantic," she said with a nervous laugh. "But I'd rather not take any chances."

"We don't have to go through with this," he said, cursing the sense of honor that demanded he offer to stop right now.

He heard her intake of breath and felt his own go still as he waited for her decision.

"I want you to hold me again," she said finally and his breath eased out in a soft sigh of relief.

A lifetime of marriage hadn't taught him enough patience to go as slowly as he knew he needed to tonight. He sensed that any moment Lizzy would panic and change her mind, unless he claimed her with only the tenderest of touches, the gentlest of words.

In the shadowy darkness Brandon pulled Lizzy into his arms and touched his lips to hers again. This time he allowed himself the delight of savoring, the slow exploration of tastes and textures. His senses exploded with a clash of sweet, poignant memory and glorious reality. As slowly and inevitably as the passage of time, he felt her hesitancy become bold desire.

And still he moved cautiously, allowing the weight of her breast to fill his hand, allowing his fingers to skim lightly over the sensitive nipple that had peaked despite layers of fabric. She moaned at the teasing, eyes closed as she gave herself up to his caresses.

"You're so responsive," he murmured. "Sometimes I ached to experience that again and I envied the man who'd replaced me in your life."

"I never expected to feel like this again," she admitted, meeting his gaze. "Thank you for that."

"No," he whispered. "Don't thank me. Just love me as you did that night."

Each touch after that became an echo of one that had gone before. Their bodies responded in harmony, as if they'd been made to fit together. Brandon didn't feel old in Lizzy's embrace. He felt rejuvenated, more passionate than ever before, more determined than ever not to sacrifice what they had found.

He did everything he could to see that she felt the same. The woman who came apart in his arms, the woman whose tears spilled onto his burning flesh was as spirited and as passionate as the one he'd held decades earlier.

Experience and time had taught them to be bolder, more demanding lovers. Love had taught them to give as much as they received.

As they lay in each other's arms, exhausted, sated, Brandon thought he had never known such joy or peace of mind. His fingers skimmed across her flesh, then halted at the locket that lay between her breasts. He heard her breath catch as he traced the shape and realized then that she was wearing the one piece of jewelry she had accepted from him years before.

"Why would you still have this, if you didn't care?" he murmured.

"I never said I didn't care."

"Have you always worn it?"

"No."

"But you did save it," he said in what sounded like an accusation. "Is my picture still inside?"

"Yes."

"Doesn't that tell you something, Lizzy? You can't mean to walk away from this," he said finally. "You can't."

He felt another hot tear spill onto his chest, and he propped himself up on one elbow to gaze down at the woman in his arms. "Why are you crying?" he asked, wiping away the tears.

"Because you're wrong," she whispered in a voice that broke. "I must walk away."

Though she seemed to choking back a sob, there was no mistaking the stubborn finality in her eyes. Brandon felt his heart grow cold. "You mean that, don't you?"

She nodded, not looking at him. Then she lifted her gaze to his and said, "But it will break my heart."

Chapter Nine

There were times over the next few days when Brandon wondered how he'd ever gotten home from Lizzy's hotel that night. He'd risked everything on the hope that once they had made love again she would never walk away.

He should have known better. If she hadn't consented to marry him when they'd been wildly in love in their teens and she'd been an innocent virgin, she would never give in so easily now.

She had always been far stronger than he'd realized, perhaps even than she herself realized. Whatever was driving her back to California was not something he knew how to combat. She'd allowed him a peek inside her heart, but he knew nothing of her soul. She'd kept that part of herself private—a secret she wouldn't share, even with him. He'd left her room feeling a depth of sorrow and regret that matched the grieving he'd done for Grace and had hoped never to experience again.

Despite that, he called in the morning, intending one last-ditch attempt to persuade her to stay or, at the very least, to wrench a truthful explanation from her. But she had left already, without a note, without a goodbye.

Brandon thought back to another time when Lizzy had refused him in much the same way. Perhaps he'd been naive to expect a seventeen-year-old girl to make a lifetime commitment to a man she'd known only days. Yet he'd known in a matter of minutes that she had brought an inexplicable, heart-stopping excitement into his life.

Because he hadn't considered himself a man prone to sentiment at that time, he'd been stunned to learn that he was capable of such deep emotions. The discovery was especially unsettling since only moments before, he'd been anticipating the hero's welcome that would await him after the war and wondering how many women it might allow him to charm into his bed. In the blink of an eye an encounter with a dazzling, barefooted girl had changed all that. He'd been able to imagine no one in his life except Lizzy.

Up until the moment when she'd turned down his proposal on the eve of his departure for England, he'd been convinced she'd felt the same rare magic. Nothing she'd said back then had made a bit of sense, either. That's when he'd first realized that Lizzy had a stubbornness that matched his own. It had made her all the more appealing.

But that was then and this was now. All he felt now was anger and betrayal. Brandon swore he would never give her the chance to hurt him again. There would be no flood of flowers, no Belgian chocolates, no pleas, no coaxing. She had made her choice, for whatever reason, and he would honor it. He'd grown far too weary of challenges.

Instead Brandon ranted and raved at everyone else, making their lives a living hell. He dropped his plans to retire, offering no explanation. He filled up the lonely hours of each and every evening with work, littering Kevin's desk and Jason's with the memos he spent the night writing. When Sammy came around, eager to learn more about Halloran textiles, Brandon even chased him off with his foul temper.

The next day at the plant he overheard Sammy telling Dana about the encounter.

"Something's wrong with Grandpa Brandon," Sammy said, clearly worried. "He wouldn't even talk about that new silk stuff when I asked him. You think maybe he's sick?"

Just out of sight, Brandon listened in dismay, knowing he owed the boy an apology. Aside from Dana, Sammy hadn't had a lot of people in his life he could count on. Brandon considered himself lucky to be one of them. Now, because of his own bleak outlook, he was letting Sammy down, and Dana was put in the awkward position of trying to make excuses for him.

"I'm sure he didn't mean to cut you off," she said. "I have a pretty good idea what's troubling him, and it doesn't have anything to do with you. This moping around has gone on long enough, though. I intend to talk to him."

Guilty over having eavesdropped, and guiltier yet over the way he'd yelled at Sammy to leave him be, Brandon went back to his office and tried to figure out how the devil he was going to get his life in order before everyone around him formed a lynch mob.

He was prowling around his office when Dana sashayed in. She looked as if she were just itching for a fight. She ignored his forbidding scowl and settled into the chair opposite his desk. It was obvious she had no intention of being scared off, but that didn't stop him from trying.

"What do you want?" he grumbled in a tone meant to intimidate. He stood towering over her as he asked.

"The truth," she said without blanching the way he'd have liked.

"About what?"

"Whatever's bugging you."

"Who says anything is bugging me?"

"Are you suggesting old age has suddenly made you crotchety?"

"Could be," he said, though he was suddenly fighting an unexpected grin. She was a tough one, all right. Just like Lizzy, he thought before he could stop himself. He moved to the window and stared out at the dreary April day that mirrored his mood.

"You weren't acting old when I saw you dancing a couple of weeks back," she commented idly. "I believe that was the lambada you and Elizabeth were trying."

Surprise and dismay left Brandon openmouthed. He turned to glower at her. "You were spying on me?"

"I was not," she retorted emphatically. "I stopped over to pick up that baby cradle you told me was in the attic. Mrs. Farnsworth let me in and said you'd gone out for the evening. I didn't even know you'd come home until I was on my way out. I started to say hello and then I realized you weren't alone."

"So you spied," he repeated.

She grinned. "Call it whatever you want. It was pretty interesting stuff. I didn't stick around for the finale, though. I left when things started heating up."

"Thank goodness for small favors."

"You still haven't said—is she the reason you've been in this funk? Has Elizabeth gone back to California?"

He considered lying to protect his privacy, then didn't see the use of it. Dana was too smart to buy a small fib, and he had too much integrity to offer a blatant lie. She'd obviously figured it out, anyway.

"Yes," he muttered finally.

"When do you plan to visit her?"

"I don't."

"Why on earth not?"

"She won't have it."

"Why?" she asked, sounding every bit as astonished and confused as he felt.

Relieved to have someone to talk to, someone who wasn't likely to laugh in his face or to make judgments, he cleared a spot on the sofa, tumbling bolts of fabric onto the floor, and sat down. Then he told Dana the whole sad story—at least as much as he understood of it.

"She said no," he concluded. "Again."

"And you're just giving up," she retorted in a tone that was part disbelief, part accusation. "Again."

"No," he said, but further denial died on his lips. "I can't go chasing all over the countryside for her."

"I don't see why not. You were planning to chase all over the world with her. Why not start in California?"

"I won't settle for less than marriage this time and she won't hear of that."

"Then I guess you'll just have to be more persuasive. Lord knows, you didn't give up on Jason and me or on Lacey and Kevin," she said. "You know what your trouble is? You're too used to getting your own way without a fight. Maybe this Lizzy of yours is smarter than you think. Maybe she sees that it'll do you good to have to work for something for a change. Maybe she needs to know she's worth fighting for this time."

Recognizing the wisdom and clinging to the tiny shred of hope in what she'd said, Brandon stood and scooped his granddaughter-in-law up in a bear hug.

"Damn, I did right by Jason when I picked you," he said with satisfaction. "My grandson is one very lucky man. I hope he knows that."

"I remind him all the time."

"I think I'll just stop by his office and tell him myself. At the same time I'll tell Kevin that I'm leaving the two of them in charge. I'm officially retiring as of today. Tonight I'll pack my bags, and in the morning I'll take the first flight to California. Don't you dare have that baby while I'm gone," he warned.

"I wouldn't dream of it. I promise," she said.

The next morning Brandon dug the detective's report out of his desk at home and made note of all the pertinent addresses and phone numbers—Lizzy's and those of her daughters. Then, his step lighter than it had been in days, he left for the airport. He refused to even consider the possibility that Lizzy wouldn't see him when he got there.

"Mother, what are you doing here?" Ellen asked when she walked into her own kitchen and found Elizabeth sitting there, staring out the window at the rain, a pile of socks on the table in front of her.

Elizabeth avoided her daughter's gaze.

"Not that I'm not glad to see you," Ellen added hurriedly as she plunked her bag of groceries onto the counter and dropped a kiss on her mother's cheek. She shrugged out of her raincoat, then ran her fingers through her short sandy hair. The damp strands fell back into enviable waves.

Finally she sat down across from Elizabeth, her expression worried. "Are you okay?"

"Of course I'm okay. I'm just darning Jake's socks," Elizabeth said defensively, picking up another pair of her son-in-law's heavy athletic socks from the stack of laundry. She reached for needle and thread.

"Why on earth would you be doing that?"

"It needs to be done."

Ellen plucked the socks from Elizabeth's hands and tossed them into the garbage. "It does not need to be done. You're bored, Mother. You've been restless ever since you got back from Boston and you haven't said a word about Brandon Halloran. I haven't wanted to press before, but enough is enough. Did something go wrong between you two? I thought you stayed on because you were having such a wonderful time."

"It was okay," she said, feeling heat climb into her cheeks at the memory of that last night. That was the second time in her life she'd made a dreadful mistake with Brandon. It had taken her decades to get over the first time. She didn't have decades left this time.

"Just okay?" Ellen asked, reaching for the teapot Elizabeth had filled and set in the middle of the table. She poured them both a cup of tea.

Elizabeth met her daughter's intense gaze and sighed heavily. "No," she admitted reluctantly. "It was more than okay."

"And?"

"And what?" she snapped, sitting her cup down so hard that tea sloshed onto the table. She ignored the mess and reached for another sock. "Why are you so interested, anyway?"

"Because when you left for Boston, there was a sparkle in your eyes and a spring in your step. When we talked on the phone, you sounded excited, alive. Now you look as though you've lost your best friend, and you sound perfectly miserable. To top it off, you're darning socks, something no one in this family has done since I was a child. Even then you only did it when you were angry or distraught," Ellen said bluntly.

"Now if that man did something to upset you, I want to know about it."

Elizabeth hesitated, then finally blurted, "He asked me to marry him."

She dared a glance at her daughter. Ellen's mouth dropped open. The next instant she was on her feet, enveloping her mother in a hug. Elizabeth endured the embrace stiffly.

"He asked you to marry him?" Ellen said, barely containing her exuberance. Her blue-green eyes sparkled. "Mother, why didn't you say something sooner? That's wonderful. When's the wedding? Does Kate know? Penny will go nuts. She said you were probably...well, never mind what Penny said. I should have washed her mouth out with soap."

"Penny is entirely too precocious. Besides, I turned him down."

Looking stunned, Ellen sat back down and simply stared at her. "Why would you do that? Weren't the sparks still there, after all? They must have been for him if he wants to get married. I could have sworn they were there for you, as well."

"Oh, yes," she admitted reluctantly. "The sparks were there."

"Then what happened? Why did you say no?"

"It was a little frightening," she explained. "Brandon can be a bit overpowering when he sets his mind to something."

"Which is what you always said you wanted. Dad let you run the show."

"Don't criticize you father, Ellen," she said sharply. "He was a good man."

"Oh, for heaven's sake Mother, I never said he wasn't. But you know what I said is true. He gave in to you on everything. I always thought you would have been better off with a man who would stand up to you. Now what's the real reason you said no to Brandon Halloran? You weren't worried about our reaction, were you?"

Elizabeth picked up her cup of tea, then set it back down. She wished more than anything that she could have this same conversation with Kate, so she could say everything that was on her mind. But, ironically, Kate was the one who wouldn't understand and the only one she could tell.

"Not exactly, but I couldn't go off and leave all of you," she said eventually, giving the truth a wide berth.

Ellen moved her chair closer to Elizabeth and took her hand. "Mom, are you sure that's not just an excuse? How often do you see us, anyway? I know we're all in the same city, but the only times we get together as a whole family are holidays. We could still manage that."

"But now I know you're just a phone call away."

Ellen grinned at her. "There are airplanes. We still would be a phone call away."

"I couldn't just drop in like this."

"Which you haven't done in months. You're usually too busy. You've spent more time here moping around since you got back, than you did in the entire six months before you left."

"I guess that's true."

Ellen's expression grew puzzled. "Mother, don't you want to marry him?"

Elizabeth took a deep breath, then met her daughter's gaze evenly. "More than anything," she said before she could stop herself.

"Then I say go for it."

"But there are things you don't know," she began, her voice trailing off helplessly. Things she could never tell her.

"What things?"

She shook her head, knowing she'd already said far too much. "Never mind. I'm just prattling on. I made my decision. I'll just have to learn to accept it."

"Mother, you're not making a bit of sense."

"Nobody ever said love made sense," she observed.

They both jumped at the sudden pounding on the front door. It was interspersed with the impatient ringing of the doorbell.

"What on earth?" Ellen muttered as she went to get it. "I suppose Penny must have forgotten her key."

But it wasn't Penny. Even from the kitchen Elizabeth could hear enough to send panic racing through her. There was no mistaking the gruff timbre of Brandon's voice.

"Oh my Lord," she whispered, wishing she could flee out the back door. He'd come. He'd actually come all the way to California for her, even though he'd sworn he wouldn't.

And he'd met Ellen, she realized with sudden, heart-stopping fear. My God, he'd met her daughter. She could practically feel the color drain from her cheeks as she stood up, uncertain whether to run to him or hide.

"Elizabeth," he said softly from the doorway, his voice a low command.

Just hearing him did astonishing things to her insides. Drawing on all her reserves of strength, she faced him sternly, wanting him gone, out of the house before he ruined everything. Even so, she couldn't help noting his haggard face, the glint of determination in his eyes—both were equally worrisome.

"Why have you come? You know I don't want you here," she said, her voice trembling with anger and frustration.

"I don't believe you. For just an instant, before you caught yourself, I could see the expression in your eyes. It wasn't dismay, Lizzy. It was longing."

"That's ego and imagination talking," she said, dismissing them. "Please, Brandon. Leave now. I meant what I said in Boston. It would never work between us."

"I'm not leaving without you," he said stubbornly. "I've made up my mind. You just might as well accept it."

She was as certain that he meant that as she was of the next sunset. Knowing that and desperate to have him out of Ellen's house, she snatched up her bag.

"Have it your way, then," she said grudgingly and marched through the house. "Dear, we'll be going now," she told her daughter.

"It was a pleasure meeting you, Mr. Halloran," Ellen said at the door. "I hope we'll see more of you while you're in town."

"Believe me, I would love to get to know you, as well," he said. "I've heard a lot about you from your mother."

Elizabeth brushed past the two of them and hurried down the sidewalk to her car. Brandon's fancy rental car was parked right behind the small economy car she'd owned for five years. She turned back just once and saw that Ellen was watching them go with an expression of satisfaction on her face.

If only she knew, Elizabeth thought. If only they both knew.

But they couldn't and that was that, she thought with a sigh of resignation. She would not destroy her daughter's life, not even for a few years of happiness for herself. The secret she'd kept all these years was so explosive it might destroy that prospect for happiness, as well.

Without another word, Brandon climbed into his own car and followed Elizabeth home. For one wild instant she wished she had the evasive skills of some TV criminal, who could skid around corners and lose the police car following. The effort would be wasted, anyway. If Brandon had tracked her to Ellen's house, then surely he could find her own.

As she drove up in front of the small stucco house with its red-tiled roof and pink bougainvillea climbing up the sides, she tried visualizing it through Brandon's eyes. It came up wanting, especially when stacked against that lovely, roomy old mansion he owned in Boston.

Once inside, he stalked through her house so possessively, she wondered if she'd ever be able to forget his presence here. He paused in front of a credenza on which there were pictures of both her daughters and all the grandchildren. The photo he lingered over, though, was the one of her on her wedding day.

"I always imagined you just this way," he said regretfully. His gaze met hers. "You were a beautiful bride, Lizzy. David Newton was a lucky man."

"I was the lucky one," she said staunchly.

He went back to studying the pictures one by one, picking them up and gazing at them, his expression sad. He put the one of Ellen back last and turned to face her.

"I've made up my mind to something, Lizzy. You might as well know it up front."

"What?" she said nervously.

"I won't leave California without you," he said.

"I suppose I owe this visit to that detective, too."

"He did supply the addresses, if that's what you mean."

For the first time, she viewed the detective's invasion of her privacy as something less than romantic. "What else did he tell you?" she asked, a note of alarm in her voice.

"That was the gist of it," Brandon said, regarding her with an expression of puzzlement. "Why?"

To cover her anxiety she injected an edge of sarcasm into her tone. "I just wondered if he'd bothered to include the color of my wallpaper and made a note of the salon where I get my hair done."

"No, Lizzy," Brandon said impatiently. "Now stop trying to change the subject. Are you going with me or am I staying here?"

Her heart thumped harder with a beat that was surely as much anticipation as panic. She couldn't afford the eagerness. "You have to leave, Brandon. Alone. This is pure craziness. I can't just pick up and go traveling at the drop of a hat." She ignored the implied marriage proposal entirely.

"I don't see why not."

"Because I have responsibilities, a family."

"You're making up excuses, Lizzy. I wonder why? What are you so afraid of? Are you worried you will fall in love with me again, and then I'll disappear like before? I can promise you that won't happen. What I want for us means taking a risk, I know, but isn't that better than leading a lonely, solitary existence? Surely you feel something for me, enough to make a commitment, enough to build on."

Of course she did, she thought miserably. But that changed nothing for her. She had to deny her heart in favor of cool logic. "Brandon, what makes you so sure you know what I feel? No matter what you want to believe, I'm not the same silly girl you once knew."

He regarded her with an intensity that made her blood race. "Maybe not," he conceded. "But that daughter of yours didn't throw me out. In fact, she acted downright glad to see me. That must mean you've spoken of me favorably. I'll take that as a promising start."

The man had always had the perceptiveness of a clairvoyant, she thought dully. How could she convince him to go, when he read her so easily?

She weighed her options, then drew in a deep breath. "I told you before, Brandon. I'm willing to compromise. I'll travel with you, if you wish. I'll visit you in Boston as often as you like. But I won't marry you and

I don't want you here." She recited the conditions as if they'd been etched in her mind, then waited for the explosion of impatience.

Instead he nodded slowly. "Okay," he said, his agreement coming far too readily. "I can see we're going to have to do this your way. We'll go to New Mexico to start with. There's a place there I've been wanting to visit. Pack your bags, woman. I'll call the airlines."

Despite herself, Elizabeth felt the dull pain in her chest begin to ease. A few days, she thought all too eagerly. She would have a few more days with Brandon before she did what had to be done and let him go.

Chapter Ten

Brandon hadn't expected to win quite so easily. On the flight from Boston to Los Angeles, he'd come up with an entire arsenal of arguments to convince Lizzy to marry him or at the least to take off on an adventure with him. That she herself had again suggested they go away together delighted him. It didn't, however, erase his confusion over what the devil made her tick.

Now, more than ever before, he was puzzled by her almost panicky determination to keep him away from California. He had the sense she would have agreed to follow him to Timbuktu, if it had meant catching an earlier flight away from her home.

Brandon waited until they'd reached Albuquerque, settled into very proper, separate rooms in a hotel and found a lovely restaurant that served fiery Mexican food before he dared to broach the subject. Even then he took a circuitous route.

As he sipped a glass of fruity sangria, he studied the woman seated across from him, her blue eyes luminous in the candlelight, her gray hair softly feathering around her face.

"Having fun so far?" he asked.

Elizabeth smiled at him, clearly amused by his obvious impatience and his need for reassurance. "Brandon, we've only been gone a few hours. What do you expect me to say? The flight was smooth. The hotel seems quiet and clean. This salsa is the best I've ever eaten. Unless you want me to praise your tipping technique, I don't know what more I can say about the trip so far."

He chuckled. "Okay, make fun of me, but I'm damned proud of my tipping technique," he said. "I can calculate the proper percentage in no time. I can manage it in at least a half dozen foreign currencies as well."

"Then I assure you I'll praise your technique lavishly the next time the matter comes up, along with any of the other experiences we share."

He reached across the wooden table and rested his hand on top of hers. Gazing deep into her eyes, he tried to read her thoughts. He couldn't. "Seriously, Lizzy," he said then, "are you looking forward to all of this or have I simply pressured you into it by turning up on your doorstep?"

"You've done your share of pressuring and you know it, so don't look for absolution from me," she accused.

To his relief she didn't really sound angry about it. If anything, there was a teasing note in her voice.

"Even so," she admitted, "It's a heady thing at my age to have a man sweep into town and carry me off to a place I've never seen before. It's the stuff romance novels are made of."

"And do you frequently indulge in romance novels?"

"They do remind me of a certain time in my life," she said with that now familiar wistful note in her voice.

"Dare I ask if that was the time you and I first spent together?"

"I suspect you'd dare just about anything. Don't fish for compliments, Brandon. You know I remember those days just as vividly as you do." A nostalgic note crept into her voice. "There is nothing in a woman's life quite like falling in love for the first time. If you'd asked me a few months ago if I would ever have the chance to recapture those feelings, even in some small measure, I'd have told you no."

"Do you regret my finding you, Lizzy? Has it been . . ." He searched for the right word, the one that captured the impression he had of her nervousness. "Has it been difficult for you?"

Her gaze rose and collided with his. "Why would you ask that?"

More than the question itself, the tone of her response bordered on panic, it seemed to him, confirming what he'd guessed. "I asked because it's been obvious from the start that you don't want me around your family. Is that because you never told them about me?"

At first she looked at a loss for an answer. Finally she said, "It's not easy admitting to your children that you might have feet of clay."

"Then you think of that time in your life as a mistake?" he prodded.

"Not a mistake exactly, but it was certainly an indiscretion. Neither of us were thinking clearly. We didn't have a bit of regard for the consequences."

"No. We were thinking more of life and death, more of love, than we were of the repercussions. I can't deny that. We might have been too impetuous, but our actions were rooted in love, Lizzy. Nothing less." He paused. "At least for me."

She sighed. "You're so sure of that, Brandon. Have you never doubted what we felt? Have you never once thought that maybe we were just caught up in all the drama of your leaving to fight overseas? We wouldn't have been the only couple to rush headlong into romance, thinking that there might be no tomorrow. Maybe it was nothing more than infatuation.''

''No,'' he said with absolute certainty. ''I think the fact that we are here together now proves the point. We have always held a place for each other in our hearts, even when we thought our paths might never cross again.'' He regarded her intently. ''Or am I presuming too much?''

''No,'' she said softly and with a trace of reluctance. ''I suppose I could deny it, but what would be the point? You may take far too many things for granted, but that's not one of them.''

''You aren't feeling guilty because of that, are you?''

''Guilty? What on earth would I have to feel guilty about?'' Elizabeth asked.

The denial was adamant, her tone clipped. Even more telling was the fact that her gaze slid away from his in a way that confirmed the very point he was making, despite her contradictory words.

Brandon deliberately shrugged with casual indifference, though he was filled with questions. ''From my point of view, you've done nothing to feel guilty about. I'm not so sure, though, that you don't feel that you shortchanged David Newton in some essential way.''

Again the response was lightning quick—too quick to Brandon's way of thinking.

"He never felt that way," she said.

He scooped up her hand and held it tight. Again, as they always were when she was most nervous, her fingers were like ice as they laced through his. Still he pressed her, ignoring the increasingly anxious expression in her eyes. He had this feeling that they were finally getting close to the truth. He sensed if he could just find the right question, he would unlock this mysterious attitude of hers that taunted him.

"I'm not talking about how David Newton felt, Lizzy. How did you feel? Are you feeling the weight of his blame even now for being here with me? Who are you cheating by being here tonight, sharing a full moon and a glass of sangria on this terrace, rather than being home alone?"

"No one," she said emphatically, but she withdrew her hand and covered the nervous gesture by quickly picking up her glass. "It's not as though we're doing anything immoral, for goodness' sake. I never thought of it that way even back then. It felt right to be with you from the very beginning."

"And now?"

"I'm not so sure I can describe the way it feels now."

"But not quite so right?" he said a little sadly. "Why not, Lizzy? What's changed? Now we have all the time in the world to get to know each other, to share adventures. No one will begrudge us that. Our children are grown. They don't need us anymore, despite what we

may tell ourselves to feel useful. We've had full, satisfying careers. These are our precious golden years. It's
time to live every minute to the fullest. Why can't you
just relax at last and enjoy every experience?''

"I can't explain it,'' she evaded again, her gaze skit-
tering away from his.

"Can't or won't,'' he pressed. "Is there something
you're hiding from me, Lizzy? Something you fear I'll
discover if we spend too much time together?''

"No, of course not,'' she said in a rush of words that
came out sounding far more nervous than convincing.
She snatched up her purse and scooted from the booth
as if she couldn't wait to escape. "I believe I'll visit the
powder room before they bring our dinner. Will you
excuse me, Brandon?''

He wanted to tell her no. He wanted to force Lizzy
to sit right where she was and tell him what had her so
worried. But the genuine panic in her eyes wouldn't
allow it.

"Of course,'' he said, standing while she hurried
away from the table.

Away from answers.

Away from him.

While she was gone, he reluctantly resolved to probe
no more that night. Whatever she was worried about
would come out in due time, if he was patient. He
sighed heavily. Lizzy always had asked things of him
that taxed him. Patience was just one more thing to add

to the list. Holding back alone ought to prove to her just how much he cared.

When she returned to the table, Brandon determinedly changed the subject and saw relief wash across her face. Her eyes brightened, and in no time at all they were laughing together as they once had, laughing as if they had not a care in the world. Whatever dark undercurrents he'd felt earlier seemed no more than a distant memory.

They walked back to the hotel, hand in hand like a couple of kids. The sky was filled with stars, diamonds on black velvet with a showy full moon. The temperature had fallen, bringing a chill to the air. Even with a delicate, lacy shawl of pale pink wool tossed around her shoulders, Lizzy shivered. Brandon shrugged out of his jacket and draped it over her shoulders, allowing his arm to linger in a casual embrace once he was done.

"Have you ever seen such a sky, Lizzy?" he asked, looking up at the cover of brilliant stars.

"Certainly not in Los Angeles," she said dryly. "With our smog, I'm lucky to get a decent view of the moon."

"Then I'm going to make a proposal."

"Oh?" she said, sounding cautious.

He smiled at her. "Come on, Lizzy. What I'm proposing is not indecent."

"That remains to be seen."

"Quiet, woman. Let me get it out. I propose that you and I spend the next few weeks auditioning the skies in all the corners of the globe until we find one that's perfect. What do you say?"

"It sounds romantic," she said with an undeniable eagerness, which gave way at once to sober reflection. "And impractical."

"Forget impractical. We can do anything we want, remember?" he asked, turning her until she faced him. He could read the wistfulness in her eyes, then the hesitation. "Come on, Lizzy. Say yes."

Seconds turned into minutes as their gazes clashed.

"Lizzy?"

"Okay, yes," she said, a trifle breathlessly. She drew in a deep breath, squared her shoulders and met his gaze evenly, adding more firmly, "Yes, Brandon. I think we should."

"That's a verbal contract now," he teased. "I'll hold you to it."

"Brandon, tell me something," she teased right back. "Do you always get your own way?"

"Almost always, at least until I met you."

"Then perhaps it's good that I say no once in a while."

"It probably is," he agreed. "Just don't make a practice of it, Lizzy. I might get discouraged."

"Something tells me a challenge never discourages you. It only draws out your competitive spirit. Just look at the way you turned up in L.A., after vowing never to chase after me.''

Brandon touched a finger to her chin and tilted her head up so he could look directly into her eyes. "Don't you try telling me that was a test, Elizabeth Newton. I won't believe it.''

"Whether it was or it wasn't, the result's the same. We're here together now. What puzzles me is why I can't seem to resist you, no matter how hard I try. My daughters would tell you that I'm stubborn as a mule, unshakable in my convictions and a stick-in-the-mud of the first order.''

"Funny," he observed. "I hadn't noticed your inability to resist me. Does that mean if I were to try to kiss you now, you wouldn't slap me?"

Rather than waiting for her response, he lowered his head until his lips were no more than a hairbreadth from hers. He could feel the soft whisper of her breath on his face as he heard it quicken.

"Ah, Lizzy," he said with a sigh, right before he slanted his mouth over hers, capturing either protest or acquiescence.

Elizabeth felt as if the world had suddenly tilted and the ground had fallen away. Brandon's kiss stole her breath and left her dizzy. If she'd experienced the same symptoms anywhere other than in his embrace, she thought wryly, she'd have taken herself straight off to a doctor. It had been a long time since she'd known the head-spinning whirl of a man's passionate kiss. Since being reunited with Brandon, it was becoming a habit.

A wonderful, frightening, exciting, dangerous habit! How was she supposed to resist a man who considered it his duty to turn her world topsy-turvy? What possible defenses could she mount against a man who thought nothing of whisking her off to the far corners of the earth just to compare the brightness of the stars? There was clearly nothing tentative or halfway about the way Brandon intended to pursue her. She would have to struggle to keep her wits about her. She'd done that once and lost to his more persuasive determination.

She would fight harder this time, she thought, just as soon as she knew every nuance of this kiss. When she tired of the way his lips coaxed, when she grew bored with the way his tongue invaded, when she no longer felt this dark, delicious swirl of temptation, then she would fend off his advances. However at the moment, with her pulse scrambling and her insides melting, that seemed eons away.

Elizabeth was shaky when Brandon finally released her, as shaky as she had been the very first time he stole a kiss. Back then, though she'd acted bold, she'd been new to a woman's lures, newer yet to a man's commanding, overpowering sensuality. From that first instant she had known that she belonged with Brandon in an inevitable way she had never belonged with another man. She felt complete in his embrace, radiant beneath his gaze, sensual beneath his touch.

Once he'd vanished from her life, she had convinced herself that what she'd felt was no more than the product of a child's romantic fantasies. She'd given up any expectation of feeling that way again. She had settled for what she knew now had been second best. That didn't make her marriage to David Newton a bad bargain. Perhaps just a misguided one. She hoped he'd never, ever known that.

Discovering, back in Boston, that she could recapture these incredible, spilling-through-the-sky feelings had both delighted and dismayed her. While it proved, as Penny's health book contested, that age was no barrier to sexuality, it also indicated that Brandon was the one partner who was expert at stirring her senses.

Perhaps she had fled California to protect a lifetime of secrets, but the action very definitely had a positive side. For as long as it lasted, she would know the wonder of Brandon's love again. As long as he didn't press her for any more than this, she would be content, ecstatic in fact.

She was still under the spell of his kiss when they reached the hotel. Outside her room, he took her key and opened the door in a charmingly old-fashioned gesture of gallantry, then stepped carefully aside to let her enter. Her blood raced with anticipation as she met his gaze and saw that familiar spark of desire in his

eyes. She had newer, far more recent memories of all
the promises that look implied.

He held out his hand and after an instant she took it,
then started at the press of cold metal against her palm.

"Your key," he said, grinning smugly at her astonishment. "Good night, Lizzy."

Before she could recover from the shock, before the
stir of disappointment could begin, he had strolled
away, whistling under his breath. When Brandon had
been a jaunty, self-confident young airman, that whistling had pleased her. Now it began to grate on her
nerves.

She was tempted to march down the hall after him,
then tried to envision herself demanding to know why
the man had no intention of sleeping with her. Worse
yet, she tried to imagine someone overhearing. It was
too ludicrous and humiliating to contemplate.

Wide-awake and all stirred up, she slammed the door
to her room with a moderately satisfying thud. Her
only regret was that she hadn't caught some part of
that sneaky man's anatomy between the door and the
jamb.

She turned the television on full blast, soaked herself in a hot tub filled with the fragrant bath salts supplied by the hotel, then ordered a brandy sent up from
the bar. She was still muttering about Brandon's low-down tactics and getting pleasantly drowsy, when the
phone rang.

"Yes," she snapped, knowing instinctively it was him.

"Having trouble sleeping?" Brandon inquired lightly.

"What makes you ask a thing like that?"

"I was having a nightcap in the bar when I heard your order come in. Then I heard the TV when I passed by on my way back to my room. I can't be sure, but it also sounded as if you might be cussing a blue streak in there."

"Listen to me, you cantankerous old man," she began, then caught herself. Two could play at his game. Her tone was sweet as honey, when she added, "I've just spent a relaxing hour in a bubble bath. Didn't you mention that honeysuckle is one of your favorite scents?"

He cleared his throat suspiciously. "Okay, Lizzy, what are you up to?"

"Me?" she inquired innocently. "I'm just enjoying the luxury of this big queen-size bed. The sheets are so nice and cool against my skin."

She couldn't be absolutely certain, but it sounded as if he'd groaned. "I feel absolutely decadent, lying here naked," she added for good measure. "Good night, Brandon."

This time she was certain that he groaned as she quietly hung the phone up. There were a few benefits to getting old, she decided. At the top of the list was the ability to give as good as you got. She switched off the light and snuggled beneath the covers. Minutes later she was sound asleep.

And minutes after that, her dreams turned downright steamy.

Chapter Eleven

When the phone in his room rang, Brandon was shaving and thinking of the sly way Lizzy had gotten even with him the night before. Anticipating her on the phone, he was unprepared for Kevin's voice.

"Dad, what the devil are you doing in New Mexico?" he asked, sounding thoroughly miffed. "I heard you went to California. Even that I got secondhand."

"Good morning to you, too, son," Brandon said, keeping a tight rein on his own temper. He didn't want to get in some shouting match with a man who'd been warned to avoid stress. He especially didn't want to risk alienating the son from whom he'd already been estranged once. His tone mild, he added, "You'd have got it from the horse's mouth if you'd been in your office when I looked for you on the day I left.''

"So it's my fault that I have to find out from my son that my father is chasing around the country after some woman?"

"I'm on vacation," Brandon corrected. "Besides, what does it matter to you which state I'm in? I'm retired. You and Jason are in charge."

"Pardon me if I don't take your name off the letterhead just yet. You have a way of changing your mind."

"I'm entitled," he grumbled. "Now was there a reason for this call? I have places to go."

"What places?"

"I'm in Albuquerque. Get a guidebook and figure it out."

"Dad, you are straining my patience."

"I know the feeling."

"Is that woman with you?"

"*That woman* has a name."

He heard Kevin suck in his breath before he finally said more calmly, "Is Mrs. Newton with you?"

"As a matter of fact, yes."

Kevin groaned. "I knew it. I just knew it. Dad, she's trying to get her hooks into you."

"You've got that backward and we've already had this discussion once. I don't expect to have it again," he snapped, then reminded himself that Kevin's concern quite likely stemmed from having his mother replaced in Brandon's affections.

"Son, my being here with Lizzy isn't some sort of slap at your mother," he said more calmly. "I cared very deeply for your mother, but she's gone now. Nobody's sorrier about that than I am, but I don't want to spend the rest of my days all alone. Your mother wouldn't want that for me, either. If you'd give Lizzy a chance, I'm sure you'd come to love her."

"Love her?" Kevin echoed dully. "Does that mean you're planning on her becoming an important part of your life?"

"For a man who deals in bottom lines, you sure have a way of dancing around the real question on your mind. I would be very proud to have her marry me. So far, though, she's not so inclined. Now, if you don't mind, I'm going to hang up. This conversation is making me cranky."

"Me, too," Kevin said as he thumped the receiver back on the hook.

Brandon wondered idly if it was possible to disown his son at this late date. He glanced in the mirror and caught the scowl on his face and forced a smile. "Just getting a taste of your own medicine," he said ruefully to his reflection. It seemed all the Halloran men were genetically inclined to meddle.

In the long run, Kevin would come around, he decided. Lacey and Jason were far more understanding.

Dana was downright tickled to be a coconspirator. They all could probably make Kevin see reason eventually. And if he didn't, so be it. Brandon figured he had enough on his mind trying to win Lizzy over without worrying about his son, too.

The thought of Lizzy had him rushing to get ready. He hadn't been this anxious to start a day since she'd left Boston weeks earlier.

Unfortunately before he left the room he made the mistake of answering the phone again.

"Dad?"

Lord, give me patience, he thought. "What is it now, Kevin?"

"I know you said you didn't want to discuss this again, but I have to ask you one thing. You hired a detective to find this Mrs. Newton for you, didn't you?"

"Yes. What's your point?"

"Did you have him look into the sort of life she's been leading since you last saw her?"

"What the devil kind of question is that to be asking? Are you implying that there's something shady about Lizzy? If you are, you couldn't be more off base. She's a fine woman. Now, I've had about all I can take of your innuendos and slurs. Maybe it's just my comeuppance for putting in my two cents worth about Lacey, but I was wrong then and *you* are wrong now. Am I making myself clear?" he said, angrier than he'd ever been with his son.

Apparently Kevin sensed his wrath. He sighed heavily. "I'm sorry, Dad. You're right. It's none of my business."

"Thank you."

"You will stay in touch, though?"

"I'm in New Mexico, not some primitive backwoods in the Amazon. They've got phones here. I'll use 'em. Now stop worrying before Lacey comes after me for ruining your recuperation. Goodbye."

"Goodbye, Dad." There was a hesitation, then, "I do love you, you know."

Brandon felt the sting of unexpected tears. "I love you, too, Kevin. Give my love to Lacey and Jason. And tell Dana she is not to have that baby until I get back."

"She says you already warned her. She also says if you want her to delay things one second longer than nine months, then you can come back here and lumber around in her place."

Brandon was chuckling when he hung up. "I guess I'd better hurry Lizzy along, if I want to be back in Boston for the birth of that great-grandbaby," he said as he closed the door to his room behind him.

In many ways, she and Brandon were perfectly suited traveling companions, Elizabeth thought as they took a midday break for lunch several days into the trip. In fact, she could already see that traveling with Brandon would be more torment than fulfillment, precisely because she was starting to recognize just how much she was destined to give up.

How would she explain walking away when it was obvious to anyone how compatible they were? She had a natural curiosity about everything, and Brandon seemed to have an unlimited store of knowledge and the patience to share it.

Even more important, they had similar views about the pace of their days. They lingered and explored. They enjoyed a stop for a glass of wine and idle conversation every bit as much as they did a visit to some must-see historical sight. Maybe they'd go home having missed a few places, but they'd have pleasurable impressions of everywhere they had been.

Impressions and snapshots, she corrected with a trace of amusement. She'd never seen a man so taken with a camera. He'd shot a dozen rolls of film already, most of it of her.

"What will you do with all those pictures?" she'd asked, laughing as he urged her to pose yet again.

"Carry 'em in my wallet. Now just climb up on that boulder," he'd insisted, pointing out a rocky ledge. "A little higher. Yes, that's perfect," he said as she teetered on the edge with a straight drop into a dried-up creek bed behind her. "This one will be a dandy."

He'd been so positive of that, he had rushed the entire roll of film to a same-day photo shop and waited impatiently while they'd been developed. When the pictures were finally spread on the counter for his inspection, he zeroed in on his favorite, a long-distance shot with wildflowers spread at her feet. He nodded in satisfaction.

"That one," he told the clerk. "Make me an eleven-by-fourteen print. In fact, make me four of them."

Lizzy stared at him. "What on earth for?"

"One each for your daughters, one for my den and one for my bedside until the day I can talk you into marrying me."

She was stunned into silence by the sweet gesture.

"What are you thinking?" he demanded.

"I thought you always knew."

"Not always. Spill it. What put that look on your face?"

"I was just thinking what a remarkable man you are."

He nodded in satisfaction. "Good, then. We're making progress."

Some days he marked the advancement of their relationship in tiny, intangible measures. On other occasions, he anticipated giant leaps. Elizabeth liked the quiet, leisurely, undemanding days the best. They'd courted once under terrible time constraints. There was something tantalizing about setting an undemanding pace, especially with a man used to grabbing what he wanted without a second's thought or effort.

"I'm surprised with the kind of life you lead, that you don't want to rush through everything," she told him as they lingered over a ridiculously large lunch that began with a spicy corn chowder and ended with light-as-air sopaipillas dusted with cinnamon and drizzled with honey.

"I've spent my whole life rushing. I deserve to slow down and savor things," he said, his glance fixed on her mouth in a way that left no doubts at all about just what he'd like to be savoring. She caught herself licking her lips self-consciously as he added, "I'd rather see one thing in a day and enjoy it, than visit a dozen places and wind up remembering none of them."

"Have you been to New Mexico before?"

"No, but it was at the top of my list. I read an article sometime back about a small town called Chimayo between Santa Fe and Taos. We'll go there one of these days."

"Is one of the Indian pueblos there?"

"No, but there's a family of weavers there that goes back seven generations to the early 1800s. I can't wait to see how they work. A friend discovered them and sent me one of their small rugs."

She regarded him with amusement. "Somehow I don't think you're nearly as committed to this idea of retirement as you say you are."

"Kevin said much the same thing the other day."

She regarded him curiously. "He called? When?"

"Tuesday. Wednesday. I'm not sure."

"Why didn't you mention it earlier?"

"I suppose because I didn't want to get into the reason for his call."

"Us," she said bluntly. "He doesn't approve of us traveling together."

"Something like that."

He reached across the table and brushed a strand of hair back from her face with a gentleness that had her heart constricting in her chest. There was so much affection in his touch, so much yearning in his eyes.

"I'm sorry his call upset you," Lizzy said quietly.

"It didn't upset me," he said, though to her ears it didn't sound as if there was much conviction behind the denial.

"Then why do you look so sad?"

Brandon smiled at her then. "I didn't realize I did. Especially since being with you makes me very happy."

"How long can that go on, though, if your son doesn't approve?"

"Dammit, Lizzy, he'll come around. Besides, we're not a couple of teenagers who need permission to get married, much less to see each other."

Though there was a glint of determination in his eyes and an unyielding strength behind his tough words, Lizzy couldn't help but think Brandon was deluding himself. Kevin's opinion mattered to him, just as Kate's and Ellen's mattered to her. She and Brandon were the kind of people who had always centered their lives around family. They couldn't very well start denying the strength of the ties at this late date.

In the long run, though, what did it really matter? she thought with an air of resignation. She had no intention of ever marrying Brandon, so his relationship with his son would never be tested. It might get bruised a little perhaps, but it would never be irrevocably broken.

Determined to banish all dark thoughts for the remainder of whatever time they did have together, Elizabeth deliberately changed the subject. "Where are we going next?"

"I thought an art gallery," he said eagerly.

"Perfect."

At the gallery, though, she noted he seemed far more interested in a close inspection of the attire worn by the Indians in the spectacular Western paintings, than he did in each artist's skill with a brush.

That, added to the comments he'd made earlier about the town they would visit in a few days, gave her the leverage she knew she would need when the time came to send him back to Boston and for her to return to California alone.

Elizabeth thought of her argument often over the next few days, turning the precise words over and over in her head, preparing herself for the separation she knew was inevitable. In so doing, she knew she was robbing herself of the precious time they did have. The internal torment cast a pall over everything they did.

Instead of being grateful that Brandon continued to insist on being a perfect gentleman, retreating nightly to his own room, Elizabeth grew increasingly frustrated. She didn't want her last memories of him to be of their increasingly strained conversations, their fleeting, innocuous touches. She tried her darnedest to recall the precise techniques of seduction practiced by some of the more skilled heroines in the books she read. Then she moaned aloud at the absurdity of her imitating them.

"The next thing you know, you'll be calling up your granddaughter and asking to borrow her health class textbook," she grumbled to herself as she tossed and turned through another night. "Silly, old woman," she added for good measure, but she didn't feel silly and she didn't feel old. She felt like a woman who was falling in love all over again and the roller-coaster thrill of it was nearly irresistible.

The curtains in her room billowed as the dry, desert air stirred and sent its chill across the room and through her heart. Bleak thoughts of long, empty days tormented her.

"Lizzy, is something wrong?" Brandon inquired the next morning over his spartan breakfast of black coffee and the half grapefruit she'd insisted he add to his

CHERISH 179

menu. "You have shadows under your eyes. Haven't you been sleeping well?"

There was genuine concern in his voice, and for once his expression wasn't smug.

Elizabeth toyed with her own grapefruit sections. "I'm fine," she said without much spunk.

"We aren't moving around too fast, are we? We could settle in one place for a few weeks, if you'd rather. Maybe Taos. We could be there this afternoon."

"Are you sure you've seen everything you wanted to see in Santa Fe?"

"I've seen enough," he said, which wasn't really an answer to her question. "Now let me tell you more about Chimayo. We'll stop there on the way to Taos."

As they veered off the highway between Sante Fe and Taos, he began describing the small town, which was no more than a dot on the map, with an intimacy that suggested he'd been there often.

"Brandon, how many guidebooks did you read before you came to California?" she teased. "Is that all you did with your days after I left Boston?"

"No. I had no way of knowing we'd end up in New Mexico. This was just a spur-of-the-moment decision when I realized my being in California made you uncomfortable. I figured it was as good a place to run to as any."

"Then how do you know so much about Chimayo?"

"Like I told you the other day, when you love textiles as much as I do, you stumble across other people who feel the same way. The Ortegas in Chimayo are like that from all I've read about them."

She smiled faintly at his exuberance. "So this is a busman's holiday, after all, despite those staunch denials you made the other day. I suppose you'll want to adapt what you see and work it into the Halloran line for next year."

"Maybe so. I admit to having an insatiable curiosity when it comes to this kind of thing. I think southwestern style is very popular these days. Wouldn't hurt to tap into that market."

In the showrooms, Brandon headed straight for the bright room to one side where a young man worked at his craft on a hand loom that was primitive by comparison to the modern machinery in Brandon's Boston plant. Threads of darkest brown and indigo slowly formed a pattern in the beige rug he was creating.

Elizabeth found herself grinning as Brandon edged closer and closer to study the weaver's technique. He asked one question, nodded at the response and fingered the yarns being used. That one question opened the floodgate to more.

Sensing that Brandon would be engaged for hours, Elizabeth explored the attached showroom and a second one next door. She picked up souvenirs for Ellen and Kate, books about the Southwest for her grandchildren and a small rug that would fit perfectly in her foyer for herself. Satisfied with her purchases, she lingered outdoors, taking in the unspoiled scenery.

When she finally went back inside, Brandon was still engrossed, this time with the woven jackets and vests on display. Elizabeth seized the evidence of his absorption and determined that the time was rapidly coming when she would have to use it as her only weapon to cut the ties between them.

Hours later, alone in a new hotel room, she stared silently out the window and prayed for the strength to do what had to be done, before she lost the will to do it at all.

The phone rang and she grabbed it, hoping that just this once Brandon's iron will had weakened and he would come share the night with her. To her disappointment, it was Ellen's voice that greeted her.

"Hi, Mom. I got your message, but I must say I'm surprised to catch you in this early."

"Brandon and I are both morning people. We usually get started at dawn."

"I hope I'm not interrupting anything," Ellen said, her voice thick with teasing innuendo.

"No, my darling daughter. Now, tell me, what's happening in Los Angeles."

"Nothing new here. I must say, though, that I've been wondering how things are going out there. You slipped out of town practically in the dead of night. Were you afraid Kate and I would talk you out of going?"

"Not you. You're the sort who'd hold the ladder if someone wanted to climb up and carry me off to elope."

"Kate, then?"

"Ellen, we both know how Kate reacts to anything she considers a betrayal of your father. Add that to her general view of romance and she's probably not very happy with me now."

"No, she isn't," Ellen admitted. "That's why I'm calling. I barely prevented her from getting on a plane and flying off to rescue you."

"It will probably make her feel better to know that I expect to be back in Los Angeles in a day or two."

"Is Mr. Halloran coming with you?"

"No, dear. I think not."

"But why?" she asked, her disappointment evident.

"I just think it's best that way."

"Okay, Mother, what's going on? Did you two have a spat?"

"No. I just think it's wiser if we don't turn our lives upside down at this late date."

"What on earth is that supposed to mean? Surely you don't think you're too old to fall in love, especially with a man who's obviously head over heels for you? As for getting married at your age, why not? I know some couples don't because it affects their Social Security payments or something, but somehow I doubt that's an issue with a man like Brandon Halloran. He looks as if he has buckets of money."

"More likely barrels," she said dryly. "I'm not saying we'll lose touch entirely again, just that there's no reason to commit to anything drastic."

"Since when did you think of marriage as a drastic measure? That sounds like Kate talking, not you."

"Dear, your sister may be foolish with regard to her own social life, but she does occasionally have a valid point."

"Not about this," Ellen argued. "Mother, if you're having fun, don't run away from it. Surely you don't think you could be happy with one of those old geezers in polyester at the community center?"

"No. Maybe not," she said wearily. "Darling, I'm very tired. It's been a long day. We'll discuss this more when I get home. Right now I'd like to get some sleep."

"Okay," Ellen agreed with obvious reluctance. "I love you."

"I love you, too." She just hoped that Ellen never discovered the lengths to which she was going to prove that.

* * *

Brandon was wakened from a sound sleep by the ringing of the phone. He fumbled for it, then said hello in a voice husky with sleep.

"Mr. Halloran?"

"Yes," he said, his heart suddenly hammering at the unfamiliar voice. Kevin? Jason? Had something happened to one of them?

"This is Ellen Hayden, Elizabeth Newton's daughter."

What on earth? He struggled upright in the bed and clutched the receiver even tighter. "Yes, Ellen. What can I do for you?"

"I thought there was something you ought to know," she said after a slight hesitation.

He heard a soft moan, then a mumbled comment that sounded something like, "Mother is going to kill me for this."

He had a feeling she hadn't meant him to hear the last remark. He swallowed a chuckle. "What do you think I should know?"

"Mother seems to have some crazy idea about packing up and coming home."

Brandon felt as if the wind had been knocked out of him. "What? How do you know that? She hasn't said anything like that to me. We've just begun to see all the places we've talked about going to."

"That may be, but I just got off the phone with her and she told me she'd be back here in a day or so. When I asked why, she said some things that made absolutely no sense. I thought you ought to be prepared."

His heart thudded dully. "Prepared how? I can't very well hog-tie her and make her stay here with me, if she doesn't want to."

"But that's exactly what I think you should do," Ellen said with conviction. "I don't mean hog-tie her exactly. Oh, you know what I mean. Just don't take her words at face value. I'm convinced she's in love with you, but she's finding all kinds of excuses not to be. You do love her, don't you? I probably should have asked that straight off."

"I love her," he said, his voice tight. "And thank you for the warning. Elizabeth won't slip away from me, not without the fight of her life."

"I'm glad," Ellen said. "Good night, Mr. Halloran."

"Good night," he said softly. He had a hunch that Ellen was very much her mother's daughter and that they both spent a lot of time with stars in their eyes. All he had to do was figure out why his precious Lizzy was so damned determined to deny that.

Chapter Twelve

Brandon woke up at dawn with an oppressive sense of foreboding. It took him less than a minute to recall why. Ellen's late-night warning, he thought with dismay. He was grateful that she'd told him, but now that he knew, what was he supposed to do about it?

How the devil was he supposed to talk Lizzy out of going home? If he hadn't convinced her by now of the strength and endurance of their love, how could he expect to do it in the space of a single conversation or even a single act of passion? That one tender, memorable night they'd shared in Boston weeks ago certainly hadn't gotten through to her. She'd dashed off first thing the next morning as if all the hounds of hell were after her.

Tricks were out. So was hog-tying, despite its appeal to his take-charge nature. Persuasive words hadn't worked. What the dickens was left? Hell, he'd inundated her with flowers once, only to have her grumble about her allergies. He'd tried candy. He'd tried sentiment. He'd dusted off just about every last thing in his courtship repertoire. He was getting too damned old for all this mincing around. Maybe he ought to fly her to Las Vegas, stand her in front of a minister and dare her to say anything short of "I do."

Before he could come up with a plan, his phone rang.

"Mr. Halloran?"

"Yes?"

"This is John Vecchio."

His heart seemed to constrict at the unexpected sound of the detective's voice. "How did you track me down?" he inquired testily.

"Finding people is what I'm best at," the man reminded him.

"But why would you even be looking for me?"

"Actually I was doing a job for someone else and something came up I thought you had a right to know about since it fits in with the investigation I was doing for you."

"Who hired you?" Brandon asked with deadly calm. He suspected he already knew the answer, and if he was right, there was going to be hell to pay back in Boston.

"That's confidential," the detective replied glibly.

"If the person who hired you is confidential, then it seems to me whatever you learned ought to be, too. Am I right?"

The man had the grace to sputter a bit at that. "Well, yes, I suppose. Although in this instance, it was made quite clear that you were to get the report."

Brandon lost it at that. Whatever curiosity he might normally have felt was overshadowed by fury. "Well, you tell your client, whoever the hell he might be, that he can take his damned report and... Well, never mind. He'll get the picture."

"But, sir, I think he's right. You'd definitely want to know this."

"No," Brandon said adamantly, "I wouldn't."

He slammed the phone back into its cradle and stood staring at it as if it were a nasty rattler about to strike. Before he could think twice, he snatched it back up and punched in Kevin's office number. When his secretary, Harriet answered, he demanded to speak to his son.

"He's on another line," she said. She served all three Halloran men but she'd been with Brandon the longest and knew all of his moods. She tried to buy Kevin some time. "Shall I have him call you back?"

"No, you'll get him off whatever damned call he's on and put me through. If he knows what's good for him, he'll get on this line before I completely lose my patience."

"Yes, sir," Harriet said. "Is everything all right, Mr. Halloran?"

"Do I sound as if everything's all right?"

"No, not really."

"That's very perceptive of you, Harriet. Now get Kevin."

"Yes, of course. I'm sorry, sir."

If he could have paced the room with the phone in his hand, he'd have done it. Instead, the short cord kept him in place, which added to his foul temper.

"Dad?" Kevin said finally. "What's wrong?"

"You know damned good and well what's wrong. You hired that detective, didn't you? How did you know which one to go to? Did you have Mrs. Farnsworth go digging around in my desk for you?"

Kevin sighed. "No, actually the bill happened to come in yesterday. I know you're probably upset, Dad. But it's better that you know this now, before you get in any deeper."

"Kevin, I know everything I need to know about Elizabeth. I told you that before and I meant it. I refused to listen to a word that detective had to say. The only reason I'm calling you is to tell you once and for all that I have had enough of your ridiculous suspicions and your meddling. If you ever expect to see me again, if you ever expect to have a civil conversation with me, you will drop this now!''

"But, Dad—''

"Goodbye,'' Brandon said. He hung up and then called the hotel operator. "I want no more calls put through to this room. None.''

Whatever the hell his son had found out or thought he'd discovered didn't matter. He took a deep, calming breath and shoved his hand through his hair. He couldn't be at his persuasive best with Lizzy if he was all worked up like this. He deliberately forced himself to empty his mind, to dismiss the past fifteen minutes as if they'd never happened.

He could hardly wait to leave the entire incident behind. As a result, when he stepped out of his room and walked over to Elizabeth's, he still didn't have a detailed plan in mind. He rapped on the door. She took so long coming, he wondered if she'd fled during the night, and he found that more worrisome by far than any slander Kevin had intended to spread.

The door opened and Brandon's gaze took in the cool linen slacks, the rose-colored blouse, the careful makeup that made her eyes seem brighter and more compelling than ever, but didn't hide the shadows beneath. His heart ached at the prospect of losing her, especially without ever understanding why.

"Morning, Lizzy," he said and before he even realized what he intended, he hauled her into his arms for a bruising kiss that left them both gasping for breath.

"What on earth?" she murmured, her expression bemused. Her hands clung to his shoulders. "Brandon, have you taken leave of your senses?"

"No, Lizzy. I don't believe so. I believe I've just come to my senses."

"What is that supposed to mean?"

"It's just fair warning, woman. You and I have some serious things to talk about today. I figure on having a hearty breakfast and some straight answers." He scowled when he said it, so she'd know he meant business.

"About what?" she asked warily.

"Whatever you're up to," he said, figuring the enigmatic answer could take whatever meaning she wanted it to.

She immediately looked guilty, and he knew then that Ellen's fears weren't unfounded. Lizzy intended to run from him.

And, despite the way his son felt about it, Brandon intended to do everything he could to prevent her going.

Brandon certainly was in an odd mood this morning, Elizabeth thought edgily as she tried to recover from that breath-stealing kiss and the knockout punch of his warning. It was a mood that told her she'd been right to pick now as the time to flee. She couldn't withstand many more kisses like that one, not if she wanted to keep a clear head. As for answers, she had plenty. Yet none of them were likely to be the ones he wanted.

They settled at a table on an outdoor terrace, surrounded by flowering cactus. Brandon was as good as his word. He ordered bacon, eggs, hash browns and blueberry muffins. Without sparing her a glance, he ordered the same for her. Apparently he figured on needing stamina for the conversation he intended to have.

Elizabeth looked at all that food, considered the implications and felt her stomach churn. She tried to will herself to say the words she'd rehearsed again and again during the night.

A simple goodbye should have come easily, especially since she knew all the reasons why it had to be said. After all, they had parted twice before. If nothing else, practice should have made the phrasing perfect. But this one made her heart ache because she knew it was irrevocable. Brandon had put pride, love and commitment on the line by chasing after her. He wouldn't take yet another rejection.

Elizabeth surreptitiously studied him and dreaded ruining the morning. Maybe she could wait until after breakfast, she decided, furious at the weakness that that implied, but grateful for the reprieve.

What was so terrible? she argued with herself. She was putting it off a half hour, an hour at most. Sitting across the breakfast table from Brandon had become one of the highlights of her day. There was an intimacy to sharing the first part of the day with him that she knew she'd never forget.

A sigh trembled on her lips. How she would miss the easy, companionable talks about the news, the thrill of studying his face as his expressions shifted from amusement to sorrow, from troubled to angry as he studied the headlines. Even more, she would miss the lazy planning of their day.

Capturing every last memory she could, she delayed telling him as long as possible. They were through breakfast and Brandon was on his second cup of coffee by the time she found the courage.

"Brandon, I've come to a decision," Lizzy blurted finally, seizing the initiative he had threatened to steal. She desperately needed whatever edge might be gained by saying her piece first.

"About what?" he inquired, lowering the newspaper he'd been reading for the past ten minutes. His gaze locked with hers. His brow furrowed in a show of concern. "What is it, Lizzy? You sound so serious."

"I am serious. I'm going home."

The paper slid from his grasp as an expression she judged to be incredulous spread across his face. Or was it astonishment, after all? she wondered after a moment's study. Her own gaze narrowed. Brandon looked as if he'd actually anticipated the announcement, but how could that be?

"Why?" he inquired with no evidence of the fury she'd expected. Instead, he was all solicitous concern. "Aren't you feeling well?"

"I feel just fine," she mumbled, trying to figure out where she'd missed the mark with her strategy. Not that she'd wanted him to fight her decision, but this absolute calm was definitely disconcerting.

"Are you homesick already? Do you miss your family? I must say I'm rather glad mine's out from underfoot."

"It's not that," she said, increasingly uncomfortable under his penetrating eyes. This was the part she'd hoped to avoid, this intense scrutiny of her motives. She didn't want to have to sugarcoat the truth. She was no good at it.

"What is it then?" he asked.

She could explain part of it, but certainly not all. She drew in a deep breath and tried to tell him what was in her heart. "I went against everything that was right and proper more than forty years ago. I can't do it again."

Lizzy wasn't surprised that Brandon regarded her as if she'd lost her marbles. The sudden surge of propriety was rather belated.

"What the devil are you talking about?" he asked.

"This," she said with a gesture that encompassed the terrace, the inn, maybe even all of New Mexico. "We're sneaking around like a couple of adolescents."

"There's one surefire way to fix that," he countered without missing a beat. "Marry me."

She was just as quick to respond. "No," she said in a rush before she dared to consider the offer. The rest came more slowly, because she had to make it up as she went along, watching his reactions, altering the excuse as necessary. "I can't leave my family and you can't leave your work. I saw that yesterday."

"Saw what, for goodness' sake?" he asked, his expression thoroughly puzzled.

He still wasn't angry, though. She found his lack of outrage just a little insulting. "You," she said grumpily. "At that weaving place. You'll never truly retire, Brandon. You love it too much. You belong back in Boston with your business, your friends, your family."

Once again he looked only slightly surprised. "Just because I looked at some old rugs, you're ready to throw away everything?"

"I won't take you away from that." If she'd meant it to sound noble, she failed miserably. Even to her own ears, she sounded like a woman grasping at straws.

"You're not taking me away from a damn thing, woman. You're giving me a future." His gaze narrowed. "Lizzy, what's really going on with you? I've never heard such a trumped-up batch of excuses from a woman in all my days. Even forty-nine years ago you were more inventive."

"Think what you will," she said stubbornly. "That's the way it has to be. You're not ready for retirement."

Despite her best intentions, tears sprang to her eyes as she confronted the actuality of losing him. He was on his feet in a heartbeat then, gathering her into his arms. Suddenly all she wanted to do was weep and have him promise that everything was going to work out just fine. When a man like Brandon said such a thing, he had a way of making it happen. She wondered, though, if even he could perform miracles.

"Oh, Lizzy," he soothed. "I'll never set foot in that company of mine again, if that's what you're worried about. It's time for Jason and Kevin to have their turn, anyway. Now tell me what's really behind all this. No man could love a woman more than I love you, more than I have loved you all these years. Surely you know that."

"But why?" she said miserably. "Why do you love me?"

"That's like asking why the sky is blue, Lizzy. It just is. From the moment I saw you running barefoot through the grass all those years ago in Maine, something within me turned inside out. There was a look about you, such a joyous zest for living. I felt as if being around you would be like basking in sunshine my whole life."

"That was so long ago, though. You were about to go off to war. You knew you could be killed. It was natural to want to grab hold of life. But what about now?"

"Nothing's changed," he said gently. "I still see endless possibilities when I look into your eyes. I still hear bells ringing when I hear your voice. I still feel sunshine when I touch you."

The beautiful, tender words spilled over Lizzy like a cozy comforter, wrapping her in warmth. The only problem was they were based on a dreadful misperception.

Those words he'd suffused with so much love brought on a fresh bout of tears and decades worth of self-recriminations. How could he possibly love her, when she knew for a fact she was a liar and a cheat?

"You don't know me, Brandon. I've done terrible things," she blurted out, then almost died from the regret that ripped through her. She'd done it now. She had really done it. He would poke and prod until the truth came out. All of it.

"Shh, Lizzy. Hush that kind of talk," he whispered, rubbing her back.

Brandon scooped her up, then sat back down and settled her on his lap, oblivious to everything and everyone around them. She wanted with all her heart to rest her head on his shoulder and pretend that there were no problems, no reasons why they could never be married. She wanted to cling to the memory of the way the sun felt on her shoulders, the way his arms felt around her at this precise instant. Those were the memories she'd cherish for the rest of her life.

"What do you mean terrible?" he chastised. "You couldn't do a terrible thing if you tried."

She had to prove he was wrong about that and about her. There was only one way to do it, one way to put an end to this charade of a love affair once and for all.

"I've lied," she told him, slowly daring to lift her gaze to meet his. Tears streamed unchecked down her cheeks. There was no need to wipe them away, when more were certain to follow. "For nearly fifty years, I've lied."

"About what? What on earth would you need to lie about?" he said, and now there truly was astonishment on his face. "And even if you did, so what? Nothing could be as bad as you're making it out to be."

"You wouldn't say that if you knew," she said, finally taking the handkerchief he offered and blotting up the tears, only to have more spill down her cheeks.

"Then tell me," he said matter-of-factly in a tone that promised understanding and forgiveness that she doubted he would offer if he knew everything. "Whatever it is, we'll handle it together," he vowed.

Elizabeth supposed she must have known from the moment the conversation started—no, even before that, when they'd met again—that Brandon would have to know the truth eventually. It was not the sort of thing she could hide forever from the man she loved, even though she'd hidden it for decades from the daughter she adored.

Now that she'd admitted to keeping some deep, dark secret, it seemed there was no way to prevent revealing it at long last. Even if she tried, Brandon would hound her forever for an adequate explanation.

"It's Ellen," she began slowly. "I've lied to my daughter." She looked into his eyes, then away. "And to you," she said in no more than a whisper, filled with regret.

She couldn't be sure, but it seemed for an instant he might have already guessed. But he waited for her to go on. She clung to his hand, trying to draw on his strength, desperate for the forgiveness he'd promised.

"Finish," he said quietly, his gaze riveted to hers. In his eyes there was no mistaking the storm already brewing. It was as if he anticipated the rest even before she found enough courage to say it.

She knew now there was no turning back. She kept her chin up. It was a matter of pride that she also kept her voice steady. "Ellen is our daughter, Brandon. Yours and mine."

Chapter Thirteen

The tension on the bricked patio of Kevin and Lacey's Beacon Hill house was suddenly so thick it was difficult to breathe the lilac-scented air. Kevin had invited Jason, Dana and Sammy over for one last luncheon before he and Lacey officially moved their residence to Cape Cod. After the closing on the sale of this house in the morning, they would keep an apartment in the city for use during the week.

Some of the rooms were already empty. Walking through the nearly barren house hadn't affected Kevin nearly as much as he'd expected it to. He was looking forward to building a new life with his wife.

Lacey had never liked this house and Jason had lived in it only briefly. Kevin's son had always preferred the smaller house he'd grown up in, more than this one that Lacey referred to as a mausoleum. They'd kept the other house, renting it out, and several years ago Jason had bought it from them and was about to start filling up its rooms with his own family.

As a result, this day, which was winding down now with coffee and dessert on the patio, seemed more of a celebration than a bittersweet farewell. At least it had until Kevin shattered the festive mood with his bombshell.

"You did what!" three members of the Halloran family exclaimed in unison when he told them about hiring his father's detective to do a further check on Elizabeth Newton.

"Well, you don't have to act so horrified," he shot back defensively. "Dad's obviously not thinking straight or he never would have done something this foolish. Somebody had to look out for his interests."

"Darling, what is so foolish about your father wanting some companionship in his life?" Lacey asked.

"Lacey's right," Dana chimed in. "I think the whole story of how he and Elizabeth were separated and how he found her again is rather sweet. Downright romantic in fact."

"There are plenty of women right here in Boston. Women we know," Kevin argued, though he could see now that it was a useless protest. Obviously no one saw this the way he did. In fact, none of them knew what he'd discovered about Elizabeth Forsythe Newton. He was only just now beginning to absorb the implications himself. She had an illegitimate daughter, a daughter only slightly older than himself. Given everything else he knew about his father's obsession with this woman, it was possible this daughter was his half sister.

"In other words, you figured you had the right to choose for him, just as he tried to choose for you before we got married," Lacey countered with quiet calm and a deadly accuracy that had Kevin wincing. "Darling," she said, "don't you see what you're doing?"

"I am trying to protect my father from a woman he obviously knows nothing about." Was it possible though, that his father did know, that he had kept such a secret from all of them?

"He knows he loves her," Jason said quietly. "Dad, I really think we have to trust him. If he's happy, isn't that all that matters?"

Kevin tried one last time to make them see his point. "But if he knew everything—"

"Maybe he does," Lacey said. "And maybe it doesn't matter to him."

"It *would* matter," Kevin said darkly. "I think I know Dad better than any of you, and I'm telling you that it would matter."

He picked up the detective's report that had thoroughly shaken him and offered it to them. "Read it for yourselves. You'll see what I mean."

But after exchanging glances, not one of them took him up on the offer. It appeared they were all as stubborn as his father. They'd rather avoid the truth than deal with it.

"You called Granddad about it, didn't you?" Jason asked mildly.

"Yes."

"Would he listen?"

"No," Kevin admitted in frustration. "He hung up on me."

"Darling, if Brandon didn't want to hear the report, then I think we should respect that," Lacey said. "Frankly, if I were you, I'd burn the damn thing and try to forget you ever read it yourself."

"How the devil am I supposed to do that?" he demanded, then sighed deeply. "Okay, fine then. But I just hope it isn't too late when Dad finds this out. You think my telling him is a mistake, but when the information comes out eventually, I'm convinced he'll never recover from it."

"Maybe not," Lacey said gently, "but it's not up to you to deliver the blow. If your father finds out whatever it is some other way and is truly distressed by it, then it will be up to all of us to support him the same way he's been there for us anytime we've been in trouble."

"I suppose you're right," Kevin conceded reluctantly. But God help them all when the information finally was revealed. With the sort of moral code his father had always adhered to, with his absolute belief in honesty, Kevin was convinced that his father would be inconsolable when he learned the truth about Elizabeth Forsythe Newton and her illegitimate daughter.

Nothing in his life had prepared Brandon for the emotions that thundered through him at Lizzy's announcement. Shock was chased by rage, only to be replaced by a terrible, terrible sense of loss.

Brandon thought of the beautiful, gracious woman who'd greeted him back in California with a delighted twinkle in her blue eyes. Those eyes were alive like Lizzy's and the same color as his own. She had hair that caught the light in its burnished gold strands. Knowing what he knew now, he could see the Halloran genes at play.

He thought of the generous, caring woman who'd risked her mother's wrath last night in an attempt to keep Lizzy from making a mistake she would regret the rest of her life. That action bore Lizzy's sense of daring and his own determination.

That lovely, strong woman was his daughter, the daughter he'd never known, never even dreamed existed.

At least he finally understood why Lizzy had been jumpy as a june bug whenever he mentioned going to California, why she'd been so determined to keep him away, why she'd turned so pale when he'd shown up at Ellen's. Lizzy had been right to be afraid. The aftershocks from this would keep their worlds trembling for a long time to come. If this was what Kevin had discovered, what must he think? No wonder he'd been so distraught.

Brandon needed to be alone for a minute. He needed to gather his thoughts. He didn't want to say something to Elizabeth in anger. He didn't want to hurl terrible accusations at this woman he'd loved so deeply for so long. He wanted to go someplace and search his soul for the right way out of this.

There was no denying the depth of hurt he felt at Lizzy's betrayal. My God, he had a daughter and grandchildren he could claim. A daughter he'd met only fleetingly. Grandchildren he'd never even seen.

"Does she know?" he asked finally, his voice toneless, wondering if that explained the reason for last night's call. Had Ellen spent a lifetime yearning for a father she thought had abandoned her? Had she worried that this chance to have her parents reunited was slipping away? Starry-eyed and sentimental, had she envisioned a future as a family?

"No," Lizzy said, robbing him of the fantasy. Then at his look of dismay, she added in a rush, "She can never know, Brandon. Never."

"Why the hell not?" he shot back.

Her eyes flashed at his tone, but her voice was even. "Because David Newton adopted Ellen when we got married. She was just a baby. I owed him for being willing to take on another man's child. I vowed to him that she would never know. He was the only father she ever knew, and he couldn't have loved her more if she'd been his own. He gave her stability. You can't want me to rob her of that."

Lizzy couldn't have hurt Brandon more if she'd taken a knife and cut out his heart. Another man had known his daughter's love. Another man had been there to care for her, to nurture her. He'd been robbed of all that. And even now Lizzy expected him to keep the secret, to protect her lie.

"What about the truth, Lizzy?" he said, as a bone-deep weariness stole through him. For the first time since Grace's death he felt every one of his sixty-eight years. "Didn't you think you owed her the truth? And what about me? All these years, all this time I've thought there was nothing left to connect us, but you knew differently." He regarded her angrily. "Just how hard did you try to find me back then? Or was it easier to find some poor, unselfish bastard and let him take my place?''

She looked as if he'd slapped her. For an instant he was filled with regret and then the rage began to build again until he was almost blinded by it.

''I don't deserve that,'' she said just as angrily. ''I did the best I could. I was seventeen when you left, eighteen when Ellen was born. For all I knew you were dead.''

He studied Elizabeth as if he'd never seen her before. The woman he'd fallen in love with would have been incapable of such lies, such deceit. The fact that she expected him to perpetuate it simply proved that she didn't know him at all, either. He felt as if all his dreams and illusions had been shattered with a single blow. Maybe that's what came of trying to recapture the past. It would never live up to the memory.

''I have to get away,'' he said. He dragged himself to his feet as if he had no energy left for anything.

''Brandon, please,'' she whispered, her face pale and panic in her eyes. ''I'm sorry. Whatever else you think, you must believe that I never meant to hurt you. Maybe it wasn't your fault, but you simply weren't there. I had to do something. Stay. Let's talk about it.''

''Not now, Lizzy,'' he said, unable to even meet her gaze. ''Dammit, not now.''

Elizabeth trembled as Brandon vanished from sight, leaving her at a table cluttered with dishes. There went her life, she thought with a cry of dismay, even as she also thought, how dare he make judgments? Though she had to let him go, had no choice really, she resented his accusations while accepting the blame for his despair. For the first time in her life, she felt defeated.

Her shoulders shook with silent sobs, which she barely managed to contain until she got back to her room. Then she flung herself onto the bed and cried for what seemed like hours, cried in a way she hadn't since she'd sent Brandon off to war. It was much, much later when she finally fell into an exhausted sleep, only to have troubled dreams that gave no peace.

It was hours before she woke to the sound of knocking on the door. She opened it to find Brandon looking haggard and defeated. She would have given anything to have the right to console him, but this morning had taken away all of her rights where he was concerned.

"Are you okay?" she asked, thinking that in her worst nightmares he had never taken the news like this. He'd been rocked, but never destroyed. What had she done to him? What had she done to all of them?

"I'm just shell-shocked, I think," he said. "May I come in?"

"Of course," she said, stepping aside.

When he was in the room, he finally met her gaze, then took in the reddened eyes, the rumpled clothes. "What about you? Are you okay?"

"I'm sad more than anything. Sad over what you've been deprived of. Sadder still that Ellen hasn't had the same chance to know you that I have."

He sat on the edge of the bed, his hands folded together, his shoulders slumped. "I need answers, Lizzy."

Her own hands clenched, she sat in the chair opposite him. "I'll tell you whatever I can."

"Will you tell me what she was like as a baby? Can you describe her first words, her first steps?" he demanded heatedly. "Was she a good student? Did she go to college? Is her marriage strong? What about my grandchildren? How can you possibly expect to tell me everything I want to know?"

She drew in a deep breath and decided she would dare one more risk. "If you come back to California with me for a few days, I'll show you her baby book. I'll bring out all the photo albums, the old movies. If it will help you, I will tell you every single thing I can remember."

"A lifetime of memories in how long, Lizzy? A single afternoon? An evening?"

"In however long it takes."

"But you won't let me spend time with her. You won't let me claim her. You'll expect me to get on a plane and go back to Boston and forget all about her. Is that it?"

Though his wistful expression came close to breaking her heart, she whispered, "Yes. That's how it has to be."

As if he were unable to bear her sad expression, he got up and crossed the room. Brandon stood at the window, gazing out at the last flames of an orange sunset. Elizabeth found she couldn't even appreciate the beauty of the splashy display. She doubted he could, either.

"Will you tell me one more thing?" he asked finally. "Why did you do it, Lizzy? Why did you keep on lying to me?" He turned to face her, his expression bleak. "When you came to Boston, why in God's name didn't you tell me everything then?"

"Brandon, I've had years to go over and over the decision I made when I married David Newton. No matter how I look at it, even now knowing that you're alive, that you still love me, I think what I did was what I had to do for Ellen's sake."

"I can't argue with you about what you decided then," he conceded reluctantly. "As much as I'd like to think I have a right to criticize your choice, I know that you did what you did out of love for your daughter. But what about now?"

He met her gaze steadily then, holding it until she trembled inside.

"What about now, Lizzy?" he demanded again. "David Newton wouldn't hold you to that promise now. If he was as fine a man as you've told me, he wouldn't deny a daughter the chance to know her natural father."

"You make it sound so simple," she said.

"It is."

"No!" she argued as if her life depended on it. "Don't you see? If the truth comes out now, she'll hate me. She'll never forgive me for lying to her all this time. I know you'll think it's selfish, but I don't think I could bear losing her. And I'm not so sure she could stand it, either. Kate was always her father's daughter, but Ellen, she was mine. Just as Kate mourned her father's death, I think Ellen would mourn the loss of her trust in me."

As she said it, she knew she was leaving the fate of her relationship with her daughter in Brandon's hands. If he chose to ignore her wishes, there was nothing she could do about it. She simply had to trust him to reach a conclusion they all could live with.

Funny, she thought, almost unable to bear the irony, it all came down to trust again. Years ago she hadn't trusted Brandon's love enough to wait for him despite the lack of letters. Now she had no choice but to place her trust in a man whom she'd betrayed in a way he might never be able to forgive.

"There's no point in talking about this anymore to-night. I think it's best if we sleep on it," Brandon told her finally.

Right now he wanted to argue with her, wanted to tell her that Ellen would understand, but how could he make that sort of promise when his own world was shaken as it had never been before? If he was having trouble with the truth, if he felt this horrible, aching sense of loss, what would Lizzy's Ellen feel? Did he dare to turn her world upside down?

"I don't know how long I'll be able to stand the un-certainty," Lizzy said, her expression imploring him to reach a final decision now.

"I'm sorry. I don't think we'll find any answers to-night. All I can promise is that I won't do anything rash. We'll take our time and decide together what's best."

If his promise wasn't enough to reassure her, that was unfortunate. It was the best he could do. He gathered from her miserable expression that it wasn't enough.

"Don't try running out on me, Lizzy," he warned. "That won't solve anything."

"Brandon, please. I think it's best if I go back to California first thing in the morning. There's no fu-ture for us. I owe that much to my daughter and, for that matter, to you. It would kill you to keep silent around her day in and day out knowing what you know."

"She is *our* daughter," he reminded her angrily, forgetting all about the resolve to let things be until morning when he'd be calmer, more rational. "Remember, I do know the truth now. Maybe it wouldn't be right to claim her, but I do intend to get to know her with or without your blessing. When you go back to California, I intend to be right by your side. You owe me that."

Her eyes widened in dismay. "You can't," she breathed. "Oh, Brandon, no. Please don't be that cruel."

"To whom, Lizzy? You or Ellen?"

"Both of us. How would I ever explain what you're doing there?"

"That's your problem," he said coldly. "I've told you that I will do nothing to hurt Ellen. That's the last thing I want. But I believe it's always better to know the truth than to try to protect lies."

Brandon left her then, because he was afraid to stay. He was afraid that the terrible pain he saw in her eyes would begin to touch him. He was terrified that the love he'd treasured for so long would force him to try to understand, to forgive—not the past, but the lies of the last few weeks.

He couldn't allow that to happen. Right now, his anger was the only thing sustaining him. Without it he wasn't sure how he'd survive the hurt.

Chapter Fourteen

Brandon's harsh words, which carried the weight of a threat, were still ringing in Elizabeth's ears as she returned alone to California first thing the next morning. Despite his warning, she hadn't been able to bear a single second more of the condemnation in Brandon's eyes.

Nor had she wanted to put him to the test. If he came with her, surely there would be hell to pay. The truth would be out and there would be nothing she could do to stop it. She might not be able to prevent him from following her, but she would not willingly set things up for him to destroy her daughter's life.

Not that having Brandon for a father would be so terrible. He was a wonderful, loving man. But he was not the father Ellen had known and loved. He was not the one who had taught her that honesty was a trait to be treasured and deceit something to be scorned. Ellen wouldn't blame Brandon for the lies, but she would blame Elizabeth.

Back home alone, though, she discovered no peace. Elizabeth wasn't sure how long she could weather the terrible strain of waiting for Brandon to make good on his threat. When he didn't come on the next flight to Los Angeles, she took heart. When he didn't appear the next day, she began to believe that he might not come at all. That didn't stop her from worrying.

With each hour that passed, each day, she anticipated the worst. Every time the phone rang she flinched. When Ellen's car turned into the driveway, she panicked, certain that her daughter was coming to denounce her for a lifetime of lies.

"Okay, Mother, I've had it. What's wrong?" Ellen asked when she arrived unexpectedly on a Saturday morning in early May.

Elizabeth had been home for nearly a week and was still as jumpy as she had been on her first day back in Los Angeles. "What do you mean?" she asked quietly, trying to calm her nerves.

"You haven't been the same since you went on that trip with Brandon Halloran. You look exhausted. You haven't been out of the house, even to visit us. You don't call. Kate's worried that you're ill."

She was ill, heartsick in fact, but not in any way she could explain to them.

"I'm fine," she said.

"You look as if you haven't been sleeping."

"Just a touch of insomnia. I'm sure it will pass. In fact, I'm feeling rather sleepy right now. If you don't mind, dear, I think as soon as you leave, I'll go upstairs and have a little nap."

Ellen regarded her intently, looked as if she wanted to ask something more, then sighed. "Go ahead, if you're tired," she said finally. "I can let myself out."

Elizabeth slowly climbed the stairs, leaving Ellen to stare after her, her brow furrowed.

Upstairs, Elizabeth stretched out on top of the bedspread, stared up at the ceiling and waited for the sound of the front door closing. Instead she heard Ellen's low murmurings, followed a short time later by the sound of a car arriving, not departing. It didn't require razor-sharp intelligence to guess that Kate had joined Ellen downstairs.

Obviously her daughters intended to gang up on her to get some answers. Given a choice Elizabeth would have pulled the covers over her head and hidden out until they both found pressing business elsewhere. Knowing that levelheaded Kate was stubborn enough to outwait her, she got up, applied a dash of blusher to her cheeks and went down to face the music.

"Hello, darling," she greeted Kate pleasantly, as if she'd expected to find her camped out on the living room sofa looking through old issues of a news magazine. "I thought you'd be on a tennis court on such a beautiful afternoon."

"That's exactly where I will be, if you own up to what's bugging you in the next ten minutes."

"Dear, there's no reason to miss your game on my account. Are you playing with that nice young man from the law firm?"

Kate rolled her eyes. "You'll never give up, will you? No, Mother, I am playing doubles with a married couple and one of their friends who is visiting from Boston."

Elizabeth felt a dull ache in her chest. "Boston?"

Ellen regarded her speculatively. "Mother, look at yourself. The mere mention of the city practically turns you green. What on earth happened between you and Brandon Halloran?"

Elizabeth forced a smile. "Certainly nothing you need to worry yourselves about. Kate, tell me about this blind date."

"It is *not* a blind date. Their friend is a woman. I think she's in the fashion business somehow."

Fashions? Textiles? Was it possible she knew Brandon? Elizabeth wondered, then dismissed the possibility with a sigh. "Well, I don't suppose it matters whom you're playing tennis with. You shouldn't stand them up. Just run along, darling. You really needn't worry about me. I'm feeling much better since my nap."

"What nap? You haven't been upstairs more than a half hour. I'm not going anywhere without a few answers," Kate said firmly. "Sit down, Mother. Stop fluttering around as if you can't wait to get away from me. Ellen, you go make a pot of tea."

Ellen took the order more cheerfully than usual. "Has anybody mentioned how bossy you are?" she inquired as she exited.

"That's how I got to be a lawyer," Kate called after her. "I absolutely love all that undivided attention I get in a courtroom. Hurry up with that tea. I want raspberry if there is any."

"You know I always keep raspberry for you," Elizabeth said. "I'll go fix it. Ellen will never find it."

"Ellen is the best scavenger I know," Kate corrected. "Sit, Mother. You're not sneaking off on me."

"I can't imagine what you're so worked up over."

"Then your imagination is getting senile, which I seriously doubt. What the devil happened on that trip to New Mexico? Ever since you got back I've had a hard time telling if you're in mourning or terrified."

She'd never judged Kate as being that perceptive, Elizabeth thought dully. What a terrible time to discover she'd been mistaken. "Kate, you're exaggerating," she said with feigned cheer. "Naturally seeing Brandon again stirred up some old memories. Nothing more."

Kate rolled her eyes. "*Nothing more?* Mother, you are not the kind of woman who engages in some casual fling."

"Who said it was casual?"

"Well, you just dismissed that entire trip as if it were of no more importance than a visit to the dentist."

"Which reminds me, dear. Have you made that appointment to have your teeth cleaned?"

"Mother!"

"Kate, when exactly did you get to be older than I am?"

Her daughter started to interrupt, but Elizabeth held up her hand. She had to stop this now. She could maintain this cheery facade for just so long.

"Let me finish," she insisted. "I appreciate all the love and concern you and your sister are showing, but when I want your advice or your interference, I'll ask for it."

Ellen came in just in time to hear her little speech and almost dropped the tray of hot tea. Kate was regarding Elizabeth indignantly.

"If you don't want our help—"

"I don't."

"But—"

"There are no buts about it. Ellen, set the tray over here. I'll pour the tea." She might not be able to do much about some aspects of her life at the moment, but by golly, she was not going to relinquish control of the rest of it. She beamed at her two precious and meddlesome worrywarts. "You will stay for tea, won't you?"

Ellen and Kate exchanged a rueful look. Kate finally sighed. "Of course."

"I wouldn't want you to be late for your tennis game, though," Elizabeth said.

"You wouldn't be trying to rush us out of here, would you Mother?" Ellen inquired.

Elizabeth adopted her most innocent expression. "Never, darling. You know how I love to have you drop by."

For once, though, she would be very, very glad to see them go.

Brandon couldn't get the image of Ellen Hayden out of his mind. He was enchanted with the thought of having a daughter. He wanted to know what she thought, how she spent her days, what the man she'd married was like, whether she was happy.

And with every day that went by, he was more and more inclined to push his way into her life and damn the consequences.

Lizzy's departure from New Mexico by dawn's early light had infuriated him. He'd raced to the airport, intent on following her, but at the last second he'd reconsidered. There was no purpose in going to California until he'd taken the time to think this situation through rationally. He'd caught a flight to Boston instead.

He'd been back in Boston for nearly two weeks before anyone in the family found out about his return. He'd sent Mrs. Farnsworth on an extended holiday before leaving for California, so he'd had the house to himself all that time. Unable to bear the thought of seeing a soul, he'd been a virtual hermit from the moment he'd arrived.

This morning, though, he was drinking some of the lousiest coffee he'd ever tasted, when he heard a key turn in the front door. He peeked between the drawn drapes and saw Dana's car in the driveway. Walking toward the foyer, he saw her step inside. He waited until she'd turned around and spotted him before saying anything.

"You sneaking in here to steal the silver?" he inquired dryly.

She scowled at him, but he had to admit she didn't seem all that surprised to see him.

"Actually, I'm on a mission," she confessed readily.

"Oh?"

"Word has it around the office that you've vanished without a trace."

"If I'm missing, why are you here?"

"It seems to me that a man who's hurting might sneak home to lick his wounds."

He shot her a dark look. "Who says I'm hurting?"

"Your son the mathematician, who apparently adds two and two better than the rest of us."

"What the devil does that mean?"

"It means that Kevin has been trying to track you down for the past two weeks. When he couldn't find you in New Mexico or in California, he guessed what had happened."

"So why isn't he here? I would have thought he'd want to gloat."

"Actually, quite the contrary. He had the distinct impression you might not want to talk to him about this. So I was elected. Unfortunately I have no idea what *this* is. Care to clue me in?" she asked. "And do you mind if we sit down? It's getting harder and harder to stay on my feet. This great-grandbaby of yours weighs a ton."

"You ought to stop feeding it all those salty pickles and fattening brownies," he said as he led the way back into the dining room. "Lord knows what kind of eating disorders that poor child will have." He pulled out a chair for her. "You want some coffee? It's pretty terrible. I made it."

"Based on that recommendation, I think I'll pass. Could you dredge up any milk?"

"Absolutely," he said, glad of the chance to escape for a minute and decide just how much he was willing to reveal to Dana. The girl was compassionate, but he had no business burdening her with his problems, especially not a doozy like this one.

By the time he'd poured the milk and returned to the dining room, Dana had pulled the drapes aside and opened the French doors to let a breeze in.

"I hope you don't mind. It was pretty dreary in here," she said. "No wonder you're depressed. You're not getting any oxygen."

"My state doesn't have a thing to do with the lack of air circulating in this house."

"Then what is the problem? You look like hell, by the way. I never knew you even owned a pair of blue jeans, much less a shirt quite that color. What happened? Did you wash the whites and colors together?"

He scowled at her. "Thanks. It's so nice to have someone drop by to cheer me up."

"I can't cheer you up until you give me something to work with. What went wrong between you and Elizabeth?"

"Now you're going straight for the jugular."

"Did you want me to waltz around it instead?"

"Maybe just a quiet fox-trot around the edges would have done."

"Hey, I'm easy. We could discuss the weather, but we'll get back to this eventually, anyway."

Brandon sighed heavily and shoved his hand through his hair. "I suppose you're going to push and nag until I spill it, aren't you?"

She nodded cheerfully. "That's the plan."

"How much do you know?"

"Not a thing, except that you're upset and, if anything, Kevin's in a worse state."

"He didn't tell you why?"

"Only that he hired that detective and got a report that shook him up. He was convinced you'd be devastated by it."

"He's got that right."

Dana's expression immediately turned sympathetic and the teasing note vanished from her voice. "Did Elizabeth tell you whatever it is herself, or did you find out some other way?"

"No. She told me. She hadn't meant to, but I was pressing her to get married and telling her what a wonderful woman she was and suddenly it all came pouring out, like a dam had burst. I guess I'm the only one outside of her parents who knows the whole story. They're not alive to tell."

"The whole story is?" Dana prodded.

When he remained silent and indecisive, she picked up his hand and held it. "You know how much I owe you. If it weren't for you, Jason and I might not be together. I owe you, Brandon. More than that, I love you every bit as much as if you were my own grandfather. If I can help you in any way, I want to.''

He felt the sting of tears in his eyes and turned away. He didn't want her seeing how emotional he was these days, how much it pleased him that she considered him family. Then he thought of all those other grandchildren he'd never even met and his heart began to ache all over again.

As much as he wanted someone to confide in, though, as much as he knew Dana wanted to help, he realized that he couldn't share this with her. He might be angry with Lizzy at the moment, he might even be tossing around the notion of going to California to claim his daughter, but until he'd resolved once and for all the best course of action, he couldn't involve other people. He was grateful that discretion had kept Kevin from doing otherwise, as well. One day soon he and his son would have to have a long talk. He could only pray Kevin would forgive him for the delay.

There was no doubt in his mind that the report Kevin had gotten contained the truth—or a goodly portion of it, quite enough to raise a ruckus. A good detective, one smart enough to have traced Lizzy in the first place, would surely have been able to discover the rest, even if it had been no more than the information that she'd had a child out of wedlock. Brandon might be the only one, other than Lizzy herself, who'd been able to fill in the remaining details.

He hoped Kevin hadn't guessed anymore than that. If he had, he was likely to be every bit as tormented by the discovery he had a half sister as Brandon was to learn he had a daughter.

None of this was going to be resolved by him staying shut up in this house, though. The only way to deal with this was the same way he would deal with a business crisis, straight on.

And that meant going to California.

"Dana, why don't you get on the phone and call the travel agent, while I pack my bags?"

Her expression brightened. "You're going to California?"

"On the first available flight."

"Will you and Elizabeth try to work things out?"

"I'm not sure that's possible, child. But I do know that sitting around here struggling with things on my own hasn't accomplished a blessed thing."

Dana drove him to the airport and insisted on going inside to see him off. When his flight was called, she hugged him as tightly as she could, given the swollen state of her tummy.

"Do whatever it takes to be happy," she murmured. "Promise me that."

"I promise."

"Even if it means eating a little crow?"

Just the thought of trying to put all this behind him and mending fences with Lizzy seemed impossible at the moment, but Brandon looked at Dana's hopeful expression and knew he couldn't tell her that.

"We'll see," he said. It was the best he could do.

Chapter Fifteen

Despite what he'd implied to Dana, Brandon had absolutely no idea where he planned to go when he arrived in Los Angeles. He had an entire flight to think about it.

He decided finally—sometime between the awful meal and the even worse movie—that he had no choice but to see Lizzy first. There were things to be resolved between the two of them before he could begin to consider what to do about Ellen.

He realized something else on that long flight. This situation he and Lizzy found themselves in was just one more test. He'd faced an abundance of them throughout his life, and more than once he'd come up wanting.

Most had been relatively insignificant, until the one with Kevin had come along many years ago. When his son had refused to join Halloran Industries, when he'd chosen Lacey despite Brandon's objections, Brandon hadn't taken it well. He'd held himself aloof, unable to forgive what he saw as rejection, impatient with himself for his inability to sway his son's decisions.

It had taken him a long time to see that patience and forgiveness were more important than pride, that a relationship with his son at any cost was worth more than the satisfaction of seeing Kevin working at a job of his father's choosing or marrying a bride who was his father's choice.

Now, half a lifetime later, he was faced with another dilemma involving forgiveness. If he'd learned nothing else over these past lonely weeks locked away in his house, it was that he missed Lizzy desperately. Until the end in Taos, he'd experienced a rare contentment in his life again, and there was no question that she was responsible. More than passion, more than memories, she'd given him back his zest for living. The old magic had mellowed into vintage fulfillment.

And she had given him a daughter. She might have made mistakes in the delay in telling him the truth, but she'd made them out of love for her daughter, not out of any intent to hurt him.

He had a choice now. He could forgive her and struggle to grab whatever years of joy they might share. Or he could allow foolish pride and misguided anger to force him into a life of loneliness and regrets. Pride and anger wouldn't keep his bed warm at night. They surely wouldn't provide much companionship.

Brandon thought of the sadness in Lizzy's eyes the last time he'd seen her and regretted, more than he could say, his responsibility for it being there. Forgiveness might not come easily, but it was the only choice he had. He could only pray that she was as ready to forgive him for his hasty condemnation of her.

Almost as soon as the decision was made, he felt his heart lighten. The dull ache in his chest eased as if his choice had received some sort of divine benediction.

At the airport he considered calling, then worried that the warning would only make Lizzy panic. Instead he rented a car and drove on the crowded highway as if he were in an Indy 500 time trial.

Parked at last along the curb in front of her house, he drew in a deep breath, praying for the courage it would take to make all of this come out right. He saw the curtains separate, then fall back into place and envisioned her reaction to seeing him outside.

He walked slowly up the flagstone walk, then rang the bell. When Lizzy finally opened her front door, he felt his heart climb into his throat. She looked miserable and frightened. Her hand gripped the door as if she felt the need for something to steady her. And yet there was that familiar spark in her eyes, that hint of mother-hen protectiveness and daring.

"Brandon," she said after an endless hesitation. Then as if she couldn't manage any more, she fell silent, her gaze locked with his. Time ticked slowly past as each of them measured their reactions.

"Hello, Lizzy. We have to talk."

She nodded and let him in, closing the door softly behind him.

"Would you like something? Coffee? Tea?"

"No. Nothing."

She gestured toward a chair, then stood framed by the archway into the dining room as if she wanted to be in a position to flee. Suddenly Brandon saw himself as an ogre and regretted more than he could say that it had come to this between them.

"Sit down, Lizzy. I'm not planning to take your head off."

"Why are you here?" she asked warily.

"I'm not sure entirely. I just knew that all the answers I needed were here, not in Boston. I had to come."

He finally dared to meet her gaze. "I missed you, Lizzy. It's odd, but the more I thought about this, the more I wanted someone to talk to. Not until today did I realize that that someone had to be you."

Her shoulders eased some, then, and she finally sat down. "Brandon, I never meant to hurt you like this. Never."

"I know. You said it before, but I don't think I really believed it until I did some soul-searching on the flight out here. I've never been much good at forgiveness, Lizzy. Maybe when you've grown up with power and self-confidence, you start thinking that things will always go your way, that you never need to bend. I learned differently with Kevin, when we were estranged for all those years, but apparently I forgot the lesson again until you came along to test me." He regarded her evenly. "Do you understand what I'm trying to say?"

"I'm not sure, Brandon."

"I think maybe you do but you want me to spell it out. I suppose that's only fair, since I suspect my actions have put you through hell these past couple of weeks." He drew in a deep breath. "I want you to know that I forgive you for keeping the truth from me. It wasn't my place to criticize choices you made to protect your daughter and I apologize for that. And I'd like to ask your forgiveness for the way I bungled things when you told me."

Lizzy's eyes filled with tears. "Oh, Brandon, thank you. Does that mean you've changed your mind about keeping the secret? Will you go back to Boston and forget all about us?"

He shook his head. "I'm afraid that's the one thing I can't do," he said. "I can't force myself a second time to try to forget you. And the only way you and I can possibly have the future we deserve is to tell Ellen the truth." As soon as he said the words, he realized that it was what he'd known in his heart from the first.

"No," she said, her expression crumbling. "Oh, Brandon, how can you say you love me and ask me to do that?"

"Because now that you know I'm alive, now that you know that I never stopped caring for you, you will never know a moment's peace if you try to go on living with the lie. That's not the kind of woman you are, Lizzy, any more than it's the kind of man I am. The only thing left to resolve is whether you'll tell your daughter everything alone or whether I will be there with you."

"You make it sound so easy, but then what, Brandon?" she demanded angrily. "Who will pick up the pieces?"

"We'll do that together."

"And what if I can't forgive you?"

"You will," he said confidently. "In time."

She closed her eyes, as if that would block out the pain, but he could tell from the tears tracking down her cheeks that she was still desperately afraid.

"Lizzy, I will be with you in this," he reassured her. "Together don't you think we have the strength to weather just about anything?"

"There's no way I can make you change your mind, is there?" she asked slowly, her tone resigned.

"No."

"Then I will tell her, Brandon. Alone."

He nodded. "If that's the way you want it. Shall I wait for you here?"

"No. I think I'll ask her to come here so we can be sure of some privacy."

"Then I'll go for a drive. I won't come back until I see that her car is gone."

He crossed the room and hunkered down in front of her, despite the sharp pain that shot through his poor old arthritic knees when he did it. He tilted her chin up with the tip of his finger, forcing her to meet his gaze.

"It's the only way, Lizzy. Whether I go or stay, it's the only way you'll be able to live with yourself."

She clasped his hand then. After a full minute while his hand slowly warmed hers, she seemed to gather her strength.

"Please don't go far, Brandon. I have a feeling I'm going to need you more tonight than I've ever needed anyone before in my life."

It was good that Brandon had forced her hand, Elizabeth told herself over and over as she sat with the phone cradled in her lap, willing herself to have the courage to dial. Only the certain knowledge that Brandon would be back in an hour or two or three forced her hand.

"Ellen," she said when her daughter finally answered.

"Mother, what's wrong?" Ellen asked at once. "Are you okay? You sound as if you've been crying."

"I'm fine, dear, but I would appreciate it if you could stop by."

"When? Now?"

"Yes, if it isn't inconvenient."

"I'll be right there," she said briskly, as if she'd guessed the urgency without her mother expressing it in words. Elizabeth made tea while she waited. A whole pot brimming with chamomile, which was supposed to calm the nerves. Then she couldn't even bring the cup to her lips, because her hands were shaking so badly.

It took Ellen barely fifteen minutes to get there, a miracle by L.A. standards.

"Mother, what's wrong?" she was asking even before she was inside the door.

Elizabeth kept a tight rein on her panic. Forcing herself to remain calm for Ellen's sake was the only thing keeping her steady at all. She studied her beautiful daughter's anxious expression, her troubled blue eyes and wished that this moment were past, that the truth was behind them and they were starting to rebuild their relationship.

"Mother," Ellen said again. "I'm starting to worry. Something must be terribly wrong."

"Sit down, darling. We have to talk." She reached behind her neck and unclasped the locket she hadn't taken off for weeks now. She took Ellen's hand and allowed the delicate gold chain to pool in her palm.

"Why are you giving me this?"

"I want you to open it and take a good look at the man inside."

"But why? I already know it's Brandon Halloran."

"Look again, darling. Even if you had never met Brandon, wouldn't he look familiar?"

Ellen studied the tiny photograph, then looked up, her expression puzzled. "I don't understand."

"You should recognize the eyes, darling. They're just like yours."

Ellen's expression was thunderstruck as she looked from her mother to the locket and back again. "What are you saying?" she asked finally in a voice that was barely more than a horrified whisper.

Elizabeth thought of the strong, caring man who was waiting somewhere out in the night and wished for just a little of his courage, just a little of his conviction that he could make anything turn out right.

"Brandon Halloran is your father."

The locket slid through Ellen's fingers and fell to the floor. "No," she said, oblivious to it. "I don't believe you."

"It's true, darling. Your father—that is, David—and I decided that you should never know. Maybe we were wrong, but there seemed to be no point in dredging up ancient history, especially when it seemed unlikely that Brandon would ever turn up here."

"You mean Dad knew all along?"

Elizabeth nodded, worried by her daughter's pale complexion. "You were just a baby when we married," she explained. "He could never have loved you more if you had been his own flesh and blood. He was so proud of you, so proud of being your father. And he was, Ellen. He was your father in every way that counted."

"But you lied to me, Mother. Both of you lied to me. Didn't you think I had a right to know? Maybe it would have helped me to understand why Kate and I are so different. Maybe it would have helped me to understand why she and Dad were always closer than he and I were."

"That's not true," Elizabeth said, shocked. "He loved you both." But even as she said it, she knew it wasn't true. He hadn't loved them equally. There had been a special bond between him and Kate, though he had done everything in his power to deny it. And her

darling Ellen had recognized that bond and hurt for all
these years because of it.

"Oh, darling, I'm sorry. I never knew how you felt.
You never let on." She couldn't console her by ex-
plaining that Ellen was the child she had connected
with—because she was the link to her lost lover.

"I suppose I never wanted to admit it out loud." She
stood up then, picked up her purse and started for the
door.

"Where are you going?" Elizabeth asked anxiously. "You must have questions."

"I do, but I can't deal with them right now. I have to
figure out who I am." She glanced back. "Did Brandon Halloran know he was my father?"

"No. He never knew I was pregnant. Darling, none
of this is his fault. Will you be back?" Elizabeth said,
following her down the walk to her car.

Ellen turned toward her briefly, the tears on her
cheeks glistening in the glow of the streetlight. "I don't
know. It seems I don't know anything anymore."

Then, with her heart breaking apart inside, Elizabeth watched as her precious daughter drove away.

Elizabeth was still standing there, her arms wrapped
tightly around herself as if she were trying to hold herself together, when Brandon came back. He emerged
from his car and walked slowly to where she stood. He
slid his arms around her and pulled her against his

chest, where she could hear the steady, reassuring beat of his heart.

And for one brief moment she tried to imagine that she was safe in a place where nothing would ever hurt her so deeply again.

Brandon had grown tired of waiting, tired of watching Elizabeth grow increasingly pale, increasingly anxious as her daughter continued to avoid her day after day. Though Kate called regularly, oblivious to the undercurrents that were tearing her family apart, it wasn't Kate whom Lizzy longed for. She needed to hear Ellen's voice. More, she needed Ellen's forgiveness.

"Lizzy, I think I'll go out for a while," he said a week after he'd arrived in Los Angeles.

She barely spared him a glance.

"Is there anything you'd like me to pick up from the store?"

"No, nothing."

He dropped a kiss on her forehead. "I'll see you soon then."

He climbed into his rental car and drove straight to Ellen's. She might slam the door in his face, but that would be better by a long shot than this silence that was destroying them all.

When Ellen opened the door and recognized him, her eyes widened in dismay. "Why are you here?"

"I think you know the answer to that," he said quietly. "May I come in?"

Too well-bred to deny him, she stepped aside, and he found himself once again in the house where he'd come for Lizzy just a few short weeks back. It seemed as if that had been a lifetime ago.

Ellen followed him into the living room and stood nervously by as he chose a seat on the sofa. She kept sneaking curious glances at him, as if she weren't quite willing for him to know how badly she wanted to reconcile the man she had met so recently with the abstract title of father that she had thought belonged to another man.

He tried to imagine how Kevin would feel if some woman appeared after all these years and stripped him of everything in which he'd believed. Kevin was having difficulty enough simply accepting that there was a woman in Brandon's life who meant as much to his father as Grace Halloran had, a woman who'd preceded Kevin's mother in Brandon's affections.

"I think I have some idea of what you must be feeling," Brandon told Ellen finally.

"Do you? Then you're better off than I am. All I feel is numb. I keep trying to fit all the pieces together, but it never comes together right. My father, the man I've always known as my father, no longer fits. In his place there's this stranger. Worse, my mother never told me, never even hinted at it."

"So you feel as though your whole life has been a lie?"

"I suppose."

"In a way that's very much what I'm feeling. You see in my picture, there is a woman who looks nothing like your mother and there is a son. Later there's even a grandson. But there is no daughter. All of a sudden, I discover there is this beautiful woman who carries my blood in her veins. But try as I might, I can't make her fit in, either."

He regarded her steadily then, until she met his gaze and held it. "I want to, Ellen. I want more than anything to get to know my daughter, to become a part of her life. I don't expect that to happen overnight, but if we took it slowly, don't you think we might create a whole new family portrait?"

Her gaze slid away from his. Her lower lip trembled. "My mother says she loved you very much," she said in a low voice that begged him to confirm it.

"And I loved her with all my heart. You are the blessing of that love, Ellen. Don't ever believe anything less."

She blinked away fresh tears. "All my life I was told there was no sin worse than lying. The two people who told me that carried out the biggest lie of all."

"Why?" he said. "Why do you think they did that?"

She was silent for what seemed an eternity before she finally said, "I want to believe they did it out of love, not fear."

"Then believe that, because it's the truth."

"I can't."

"Why not?"

"Then I would have to forgive them," she said in a small voice, "and it still hurts too much to do that."

"Ah, Ellen," he said with a rueful sigh. "Let me tell you something I've only recently discovered about forgiveness. It's when it's needed the most that it becomes the hardest to give. You will never be happy until you forgive your mother, your father, even me."

"Why you?"

"Because I set it all in motion by searching for your mother. If I hadn't, you would never have known. Would that have been better?"

She hesitated, then finally admitted, "No. I think, if I give it some time, it might turn out that I'm luckier than anyone to have had the love of two fathers."

Brandon knew then that though it would take time for Ellen to accept him into her life, it would be all right. The healing really had begun. "Do you think you could tell your mother that?"

"Now?"

He nodded. "I think it's the only way I'll ever convince her to marry me."

A smile crept over her lips. "Better late than never, I always say," she said with more spirit. "Just let me fix my face."

"Your face is lovely just as it is."

"Only a father would say that," she said, then caught herself. Her smile broadened. "How about that? I can actually begin to laugh again. By the way, am I the only thing standing between the two of you?"

"Not the only thing," he conceded. "Just the most important."

"What else stands in the way? I knew weeks ago you loved each other."

"Time. Too much water under the bridge. Stubbornness."

"Yours or hers?" she asked slyly.

Brandon could tell his daughter had Lizzy's spunk from the twinkle in her eyes. "Maybe some of each."

Before Ellen could offer any advice, the front door slammed open and Lizzy stood there, her expression wary. "Brandon," she said worriedly. "You didn't say you were coming here."

"Ellen and I were just getting to know each other," he said.

Elizabeth cast an anxious glance at her daughter. "Is everything okay?"

Ellen hesitated, her expression indecisive. Then, after a glance at Brandon, she moved slowly toward her mother and put her arms around her. "Not quite yet," she said with the kind of honesty Brandon had come to respect. "But it will be. I'm sorry for shutting you out. I needed time to sort things out for myself."

"You had a right to be angry."

"Maybe. Maybe not." She glanced at Brandon. "It was . . . it was Father who made me see the light."

Lizzy turned to him, tears glistening in her eyes. "Thank you," she mouthed as she held her daughter.

Ellen gave her one last squeeze, then shot a pointed look at Brandon. "I think I'll leave you two alone now," she said. "There's tea in the kitchen, if you want some, Mother."

When she had gone, Lizzy crossed the room to him. "You worked a miracle here this afternoon."

He shook his head. "No, Lizzy, the miracle is you and me. We've got our second chance. I don't plan to let it pass us by. How about you?"

A smile spread across her face and her eyes lit with sparks of pure mischief. "You knew all along you'd have your way this time, didn't you?"

"Of course," he said. "You never could resist a story with a happy ending, could you?"

"Brandon, how will I be able to thank you?"

"By marrying me, Lizzy. By letting me become a part of your family, just as you'll become a part of mine."

She squeezed his hand. "I do love you, Brandon Halloran. I always have."

"And I you, my love. And I you."

"It won't be easy, you know. Kate and your family still have to be told."

"I think Kevin already knows, at least some of it. He may have guessed the rest."

"Then don't you think you should call him? He must have a thousand questions."

"I can't call, not about something as important as this. I'll stay here until you've had time to make things right with both your daughters, then we'll go to Boston together. I figure we can manage a June wedding, don't you?"

"Brandon, June is just around the corner."

He grinned at her stunned expression. "Then I'd say you'd better get a move on, woman."

Epilogue

"Ohmigosh," Dana murmured just as Brandon was about to cut the tiered wedding cake that was decorated with a frothy confection of white frosting and pink rosebuds.

"Sis?" Sammy said, an expression of alarm on his face as she clutched her belly.

Brandon heard the mix of anxiety and surprise in Dana's voice and immediately dropped the sterling silver cake knife. He shot her a look of pure delight. "Now?"

A grin split her face. "Now," she confirmed. "This great-grandchild of yours is definitely coming."

"By golly, I knew this was going to be a day to remember," Brandon said and started giving orders. "Jason, get the car. Kevin, you tell the guests they'll have to excuse us."

Dana looked him straight in the eye. "Don't you dare ruin this reception on my account."

"Ruin it! Hell, girl, this is the best thing that could have happened. Now I'll be able to leave on my honeymoon without worrying about missing the big event."

Forgetting that he'd just given the assignment to Kevin, he grabbed the microphone from the bandleader in mid-song and called for silence. "Well, folks, I guess you all know we wanted you with us on this special day because we care about you. It's a mighty big blessing to have so many friends and family around us on a day when we celebrate the true meaning of the wedding vows. There's been a little hitch in our schedule, though. I'm afraid you're going to have to excuse us. We've got a baby to deliver."

As a murmur of excitement spread through the room, he again asked for quiet. "While we get ourselves to the hospital, I hope you'll all stay here and enjoy yourselves and drink a toast to the newest Halloran, our fourth generation."

At the hospital it was difficult to tell who was more impatient—Brandon, Kevin or Sammy. They paced the waiting room, while Elizabeth and Lacey exchanged looks of amusement. Ellen and Kate hovered nearby, still awkward around their new family but clearly wanting to be a part of this special moment.

"Why the devil don't they tell us something?" Brandon grumbled.

"First babies generally take their own sweet time," Elizabeth reminded him. "I'm sure they'll let us know when there's anything to tell us. Why don't we go have a nice cup of tea to settle your nerves?"

"A stiff scotch couldn't settle my nerves," he said. "I don't recall it taking this long for Kevin or Jason to come into this world."

"Probably because you were at work on both occasions," Kevin reminded him dryly. "Maybe you and Elizabeth should leave before you miss your plane."

"Not on your life." He stared down the corridor toward the delivery room. "Maybe I could get one of those gowns and just take a peek inside to see what's happening."

"Bad idea," Kevin said. "This is Jason's big day. There's no need for you to intrude."

"How would I be intruding? It's my great-grandbaby."

"Which puts you two generations away from the right to be in there," his son reminded him with a grin that had been a long time coming.

Though Kevin had taken the events of the past few weeks far better than Brandon had anticipated, it hadn't been easy. Once Kevin had been told the whole story, he'd swallowed any criticisms he might have had of his father or Elizabeth. He had not welcomed his new step mother as wholeheartedly as Brandon might have liked, but there had been no overt resentment. Brandon suspected he could thank Lacey and Dana for that, just as he owed them for making both Ellen and Kate feel welcome under difficult circumstances. He was proud of all of them for trying to put the past behind them.

It had been most difficult of all for Kate, he suspected. She alone had no blood ties to her new family. But she was strong and independent, and a damned sight too cynical about romance from what he'd seen. Whatever hurts she'd suffered, it was time she let them go. She needed a new man in her life to spark things up. He might look around among the up-and-coming young men in Boston and see to that himself, once he and Lizzy got back from their honeymoon.

"Lizzy, have you seen the doctor?" he asked worriedly. "I didn't see him go in. Who ever heard of delivering a baby without a doctor?"

"The doctor probably slipped in the back way just to avoid you and all your last-minute instructions," Lacey teased.

Sammy sidled up to him. "Come on, Grandpa Brandon. Let's go get some cigars."

"I suppose we could," he said with a last grudging glance down the hall. He looked at Elizabeth. "You suppose there's time?"

"More than likely," she told him.

"What's that mean?"

"It means I can't guarantee it," she said.

"Then I'm not budging. What do you suppose they'll name him? Did they tell anybody?"

"Not me," Sammy said. "I've been bugging Dana for weeks, but she wouldn't say a word."

"You seem awfully certain it's going to be a boy," Elizabeth said. "Last I heard girls were a possibility as well."

Brandon shot Lizzy a pleased look, then gazed for a moment at his new daughter. "I guess they are at that," he said, just as a nurse came out of the delivery room and started toward them.

"You're all here with Dana and Jason Halloran?" she asked.

"Yes," Brandon said. "Everything's okay in there, isn't it?"

"Everything is just fine. If you'd like, you can come with me. Dana and Jason want you to see your new grandchild."

Brandon was the first one down the hall. This great-grandbaby of his was going to have a fine life. He'd personally guarantee that. He fumbled with the ties on the gown he'd been given, then struggled with the mask. He seemed to be all thumbs. He felt Elizabeth's fingers nudging his aside, then her sure touch at the fastenings.

Then the nurse was opening the door to Dana's private room. Brandon stepped inside, his gaze going at once toward Dana and his grandson. Jason was holding a tiny bundle cradled in his arms.

As they stepped closer, he could see Dana's radiant face and felt as though his own heart would fill to bursting with sheer joy at having a new little Halloran born on this day that would always be special to all of them.

"Dad, Granddad, Mom, Elizabeth, and Sammy," Jason said slowly, beaming with pride. His glance included Ellen and Kate, though he didn't mention their names. "I'd like you to meet our daughter."

"Oh, my," Lacey said softly, taking Dana's hand and squeezing it. "A girl. Darling, that's wonderful."

Dana looked at each one of them, then said, "If you don't mind, we'd like to name her Elizabeth Lacey Halloran... We'll call her Beth."

Brandon watched as his new bride and his beloved daughter-in-law exchanged a misty-eyed look. Truth be told, his own eyes seemed to be stinging just a bit.

"I would be honored," Lizzy said.

"So would I," Lacey added.

Elizabeth Lacey Halloran, Brandon thought with a sigh as he gazed into that tiny, precious face. A new generation, named for the old and made strong by their love.

Indeed, he thought, as he took Elizabeth's hand in his, the best was yet to come.

* * * * *

It takes a very special man to win

That
SPECIAL
Woman!

She's friend, wife, mother—she's you! And beside each Special Woman stands a wonderfully *special* man. It's a celebration of our heroines—and the men who become part of their lives.

Look for these exciting titles from Silhouette Special Edition:

January **BUILDING DREAMS** by Ginna Gray
Heroine: Tess Benson—a woman faced with single motherhood who meets her better half.

February **HASTY WEDDING** by Debbie Macomber
Heroine: Clare Gilroy—a woman whose one spontaneous act gives her more than she'd ever bargained for.

March **THE AWAKENING** by Patricia Coughlin
Heroine: Sara McAllister—a woman of reserved nature who winds up in adventure with the man of her dreams.

April **FALLING FOR RACHEL** by Nora Roberts
Heroine: Rachel Stanislaski—a woman dedicated to her career who finds that romance adds spice to life.

Don't miss THAT SPECIAL WOMAN! each month—from some of your special authors! Only from Silhouette Special Edition!

TSW

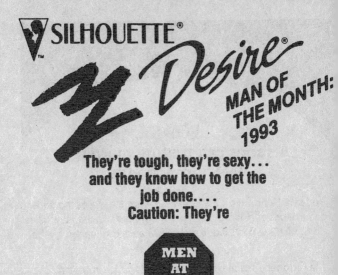